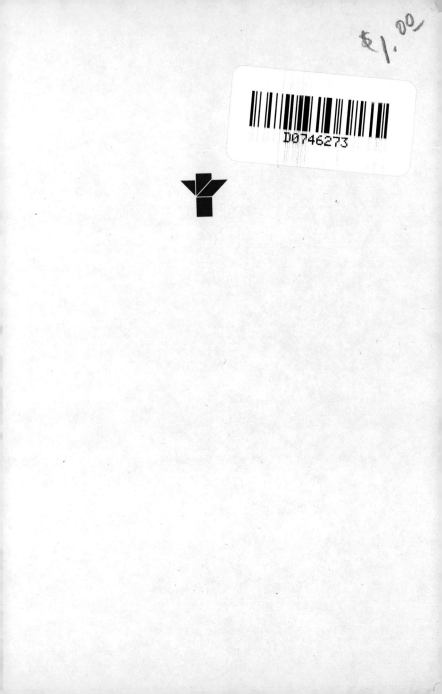

POOL

a novel

Ajay
Sahgal

Grove Press
New York

Published simultaneously in Canada
Printed in the United States of America

Originally published by Atlantic Monthly Press in 1994. Grove Press paperback edition published in 1995.

Library of Congress Cataloging-in-Publication Data

Sahgal, Ajay.
    Pool: a novel / Ajay Sahgal.
    ISBN 0-8021-3343-6
    I. Title
  [PS3569.A373P66 1994] 813' .54 —dc20   94-37213

DESIGN BY LAURA HOUGH

Grove Press
841 Broadway
New York, NY 10003

10 9 8 7 6 5 4 3 2 1

for Bret Ellis

ACKNOWLEDGMENTS

Many thanks to my parents, Shanti Sahgal and Bheem Sahgal, for their encouragement and support. Thanks also to Marvin Kaphan, Carolyn See, Brian Moore, and Richard Elman.

You walk for days, among trees and among stones. Rarely does the eye light on a thing, and then only when it has recognized that thing as the sign of another thing: a print in the sand indicates the tiger's passage; a marsh announces a vein of water; the hibiscus flower, the end of winter. All the rest is silent and interchangeable; trees and stones are only what they are.

—*Italo Calvino*, Invisible Cities

The goddam movies. They can ruin you.

—*Holden Caulfield*

ACT I

I have no idea what to think. I exhale and look up at the huge stone house in front of me. Danny is getting my things from the car and I stretch, the back of my shirt wet from the ride. Four black leather bags at my feet. Danny gets the camera out of the back and starts to videotape me. He moves around to the side of the car for a profile, and with the sun setting, I imagine I must look noble in this orange light, the dark house somewhere in frame, and if not quite noble, then something better than I am.

The house is dark, no lights on inside and Patsy Cline's playing, filtering out from an open window. The air thick and sweet-smelling, it's hot out, humid and wet, like maybe there was rain. Nothing moves. A banging noise comes from inside the house; then everything is quiet again except for the slow country song playing.

I can hear Danny's feet moving, trying to get another angle. When I open my eyes again, Danny stands on the hood of the car, camera aimed straight at my face, motioning for me to turn around. When I do, Jeremiah is standing on the front steps, perfectly framed between two huge columns.

"Are you here to help?" Jeremiah asks. "Because if you're not here to *help*, the gate's that way."

Jeremiah points at the long driveway, the iron gate hard to see in this light, with my sunglasses on.

"Where is everyone?" I ask.

"I thought you were shooting," Jeremiah says. "Anne said you wouldn't be here for another three, four weeks."

"That's what everyone thought," Danny says from behind the camera.

"Who's this?" Jeremiah asks me.

"My driver," I say, yawning.

"Don't tell me you still don't know how to drive a fucking car, Emery." Jeremiah.

"I brought my personal valet," I say.

"Assistant," Danny says. "Actually third year USC film school."

"Valet," I say.

"Thesis project: documentary," Danny says. "Subject: Emery Roberts."

Jeremiah says nothing.

"I thought this was your Hollywood expatriate center," Danny says. "People like Emery aren't allowed? Have the membership rules changed or something?"

"I don't allow any of that movie business shit here, Emery. No assistants, no drivers, no agents, no *valets*. I'm the only one with quote-unquote power here."

"Fine," I say tiredly. "Danny, you're fired."

"Can I be Emery's entourage?" Danny asks Jeremiah. "Will that change things?"

"What happened to the movie?" Jeremiah asks me. "What about the *movie?*"

Jeremiah is big, six and a half feet, muscles, crew cut. Danny jumps off the car and crouches down low, crawling forward, the camera aimed at Jeremiah, a towering figure filling the frame.

"Hollywood's three thousand miles away," Jeremiah says. "Understand?"

"Why do you think he's here?" Danny asks.

"Why do you think I'm here?" I finally ask, lighting a Marlboro.

"Leave all the attitude and smarmy shit back where it belongs. This is real life. I'm the king of the castle. No smoking in the house." Jeremiah ignores the camera. He turns around and goes inside, slamming the front door.

Danny has the camera pointed back at me now.

"I want a raise," Danny says.

"Talk to my agent," I hear myself say. "My agent . . . agreed to this documentary . . . didn't she?"

"Entourages make more money than assistants," Danny says. "One day you're going to pay me a million dollars just to *light* you."

"One day you're going to be the next Phil Joanou."

The front door opens and Danny swings the camera around.

"Who's the cameraman?" Anne asks.

"My assistant."

"Entourage," Danny says from behind the camera. "Your brother's mad at us."

"Mr. Fixit's had a bad day," Anne says. "The upstairs electricity went out. The whole place is falling apart."

"It looks a hundred years old," Danny says.

"One-sixty something. Did you finish shooting already?" Anne asks me.

"You could say that," Danny says.

"What does that mean?" Anne slurs, walks unsteadily toward us.

"He walked," Danny says. "Two weeks left on the shoot and Emery walks."

I just stand there.

"You quit?" Anne asks. "They're not upset?"

"They don't really, like, know," I say. "Yet."

Danny zooms in on me. "He's due back on set Monday."

"Bet you're going to be really popular back there." In this dusk I can't tell if Anne is smiling.

"Emery's single now, too, by the way," Danny says. "Lost his manager *and* his girlfriend in one shot."

"Danielle?" Anne sighs, gestures around her. "Why Vermont?"

Danny laughs, answers for me. "It's as far from L.A. as Emery could get and still know people."

"Emery's thinking like Jeremiah now," Anne says. "That's real advancement, Emery."

A dog comes running out of the house and sniffs at my crotch. Anne pulls it away, pats it on the head.

"You don't miss the restaurants?" Anne asks, distracted. "The Santa Ana. The blue Pacific. All that fawning?"

"Only thing Emery misses is what your dog just did to him." Danny.

I slap a mosquito on my arm.

"Sort of." I shrug. "There aren't any bugs there."

"I guess you haven't been hanging out at CAA lately," Danny says.

"It could get dull up here for you," Anne warns.

I look at my shoes. Soon it will be completely dark out.

"Dull is good," I say, looking at my feet. "I'm dull."

"That can't be possible, Em," Danny says. "Because you're not good. See—there's a contradiction."

"I'm sure your life is real dull," Anne says, her foot nudging one of my bags. "I can't believe you walked out on this job. Aren't you afraid people will sue you? I mean, Jesus, Emery, do you grasp *anything?*"

Danny has the camera off now and is getting his duffel bag out of the car. "I think you'll be getting a lot of lawyer phone calls."

"They can't call and they can't sue if they don't know where I am."

Danny sighs. "You're the boss."

Anne looks down at my bags. "I see you plan to stay awhile. Who's feeding the pig?"

"Are we talking about Danielle?" Danny asks. "The pig?"

"Emery has a Vietnamese potbellied pig," Anne says. "Named Prosciutto."

"Bacon." I sigh. "But I changed his name to Pig."

Danny scratches his arm. "Emery's lonely. It's hard giving your girlfriend-slash-manager the ditch."

"Emery's the exact opposite of lonely," Anne says.

"Or maybe it's manager-slash-girlfriend?" Danny looks confused.

"Need help with all this stuff?" Anne finally asks, turning away.

Black silhouettes against a deep blueblack sky are hills. Danny is already in the door, the dog following. I follow the dog.

Anne guides us upstairs to our rooms with a flashlight, holding a small bottle of Absolut Citron.

"Yours used to be a closet," Anne says to Danny as she opens his door.

"A manservant's needs are simple," Danny says.

In my room Anne lights candles, turns off the flashlight. There is a bed, a chest of drawers, a chair, dim with the candles, everything murky, the smell of honey.

"This will not do at all," Danny says, hitting the record button and pointing the camera at me. "Emery needs a TV, *at least* two phone lines, fresh flowers, cable, fax, Nautilus, StairMaster, minibar. I assume there is maid service. Emery always has maid service in his contract."

"There is *no* contract," Anne says, pissed. "You're guests. Be quiet. Or leave."

"In Jeremiah's strictly un-Hollywood environment," Danny says to Anne as she walks out the door.

I start to unpack one of my bags, then realize there is nowhere to put anything. Danny zooms in on my face.

I sigh. "One good thing about our relationship is I'm comfortable in front of a camera."

"One good thing." Danny backs out of the room and heads for his own.

Hammering noises start, then stop. It is hot and I open a window, stick my head out, listening to bug sounds. Someone moves on the ground below me, but it's too dark to really see a face. The shape picks up a shovel, walks over to a small hole, and starts to dig. I can barely make out an upper body, no shirt on, just digging, grunting with every push of the shovel.

The lights in my room come on. I pull my head back

inside and turn around. Jeremiah stands near the bed, his hands
dirty, holding some tools, sweaty.

"Light," I hear Danny say from the next room.

Jeremiah smiles, then stops.

"You got the electricity working again," I say.

Jeremiah nods, looks at the floor. "Anne says you quit.
That you walked off the set."

"How are you?" I ask. "Do you miss Los Angeles?"

"Are you capable of answering a question or is this the
same old Emery?"

"Anne says you're trying to fix the place up," I say.

Jeremiah shrugs, looks at the walls. "More like trying to
keep it from falling down. I'm running out of money."

"How much do you need?" I ask.

"A lot," he says. "I mean, look at this place."

I sit on the bed and watch him pace the room. Jeremiah
studies the floor.

"What do they pay you now?" Jeremiah asks. "Three? I
heard you got three extra jumbo. Your price went up since
when?"

"I don't know," I say. "Less than three."

"That's money," Jeremiah says. "Three is money. Almost makes it worth it."

I shrug, then say, "This is . . . a great house."

"Anyway that's why *I* left, right? A place gets to you, say
goodbye." Jeremiah runs a hand across the wall, inspecting it.

"This is a great house," I say.

"Are they going to sue you?" Jeremiah asks casually. "I mean, I assume you're going to be sued."

"I thought you didn't want to talk about that stuff."

"So you want to help me with the house?"

"I'll do whatever you want."

"Jesus. Actors are all like that."

I nod.

"Louis went drinking. How's his girlfriend—I use the term loosely—and the kid? What's the kid's name again?"

"Enzo," I hear myself say.

"*Sun City* is going to make Becky a big star, I hear. Louis is miserable about it," Jeremiah says. "But you date an actress, you have to deal with it."

"Is Nathan writing screenplays still?"

"Geffen bid seven hundred thousand for the last one," Jeremiah says.

"Did his agent say . . . yes?"

Jeremiah shakes his head. "Nathan's building a swimming pool."

Later, downstairs, I follow the sound of the theme from "Cheers" into a little room. Danny is on a couch, the camera pointed at the TV, at the opening credits of the show.

"What's going on?" Danny asks.

"Shh," I say.

I stand there and watch for a couple of minutes. Anne comes in.

"Ready?" she asks.

I shrug. "I'm tired."

"Emery didn't get much sleep on the flight out," Danny says. "Agent from UTA two seats in front of us."

Anne sighs. "Jesus, Emery. You're the only person I know dumb enough to try to escape Hollywood undetected by flying out on MGM Grand."

"Where are we going?" I ask. "I'm tired."

"Town," Anne says. "Louis is there. We'll meet him for a drink. You can drive us, Danny."

Danny takes out a cigarette, lights a match. "I drove all day."

"I wouldn't light that," Anne says. "Jeremiah's number one rule. No smoking in the house."

Danny blows out the match, puts the cigarette back in the box. "Fucking ex-smokers. The worst humanity has to offer."

"Drive us," Anne says.

He shakes his head. "Only if Emery fucks me."

I stare at Danny for a while until I say, "Okay."

Danny drives down small roads, dark everywhere around us, no moon. Anne plays with the video camera in the backseat, and my head is out the window, warm air hitting my face. There's nothing to see but a blur of trees.

"What's this place called?" Danny asks.

"The D," Anne says.

"What's the D?" Danny says. "D as in dumbshit?"

"What's it like working with Hurley?" Anne asks sarcastically. "Speaking of . . ."

"Hurley Thompson," I say. "I'd work with Hurley *Teen Town* Thompson for free."

"Ooh. One star who's willing to talk candidly about another star 'on the record.' "

"What's the D?" Danny asks.

"Pretty big deal then," Anne says. "Hurley Thompson, Emery Roberts."

"Hurley Thompson is five-eight." I sigh.

Anne rubs my shoulders from behind and it kind of hurts, but I don't say anything.

"What's he like? I think he's gorgeous," Anne says. "Short but gorgeous."

"Ask the producer," I mutter. "Or are you and Daddy going through one of your nonspeaking phases?"

"Monty doesn't gossip," Anne says.

"Yeah, and Emery's not lobotomized," Danny says, then asks, "What's the *D* stand for? Or am I supposed to guess?"

"I'm tired."

We pull onto the main street of town. Everything looks closed. Up ahead is a sign. It says "Dynamo Cocktails." Danny parks in front.

Danny says, "Oh."

Louis walks out the front door, and Danny and Anne go inside. Louis gives me a hug.

"You wrap early?" Louis asks nervously, drunk.

"No."

"Because Becky didn't say anything about the picture wrapping early," Louis says, blocking my way in. "So I'm assuming the picture did not wrap early."

"It didn't."

"So?" Louis asks. "What the fuck is going on?"

"Danielle and I broke up," I say.

Louis hugs me again. "Let's celebrate."

There are locals standing outside the D's door, tall-neck beers in hand, laughing at something. Immediately one of them, a Red Sox cap on, stares, taps his friends, points.

"Hey," he calls out. "Don't I know you?"

"Good evening, gentlemen," Louis says, bowing, as he walks me by them.

"You looking at something?" one of them says to me.

Louis puts his arm around my shoulder. "Nothing but a little drink. My boy here just lost his woman. He's womanless. We're going to try to make him feel better."

"I know I know you from somewhere," the guy with the cap says. "Are you from Dorset?"

Louis shakes his head for me. A townie wearing a Hard Rock T-shirt whispers to the guy with the cap on, points at me, recognizes someone.

Louis opens the door, and as we step inside, I can hear them laugh, one of them saying, "Emery Roberts."

"We're going to get killed in here," Louis says, grinning. "You do know that, right?"

The D is a dive, one room, green walls, a few booths, video games, a pool table, stools, jukebox. Anne and Danny sit at a table in the corner. Louis guides me to the bar.

"Let's get out of here," I say.

"We'll have a drink and you can tell me if my creature's been misbehaving."

Louis motions for the bartender, a big guy, beard, who walks over to our end of the bar, slowly.

"How are you tonight?" Louis says to him.

The man nods grimly, wipes the counter.

"Could we get two Sea Breezes please?"

"Make it a Sea Breeze and a beer," I say. "Corona."

The bartender stares at me blankly, impatient.

"I don't think they have Corona," Louis says. "Get a Sea Breeze."

"I don't want anything called Sea Breeze."

Stepping on my foot, Louis holds up two fingers to the bartender, who continues to stare.

"Fine," I say. "What the fuck is a Sea Breeze?"

Louis purrs, "It is vodka. It is cranberry. It is grapefruit. It is nirvana."

The bartender walks away and starts pouring.

"Last week Nathan attempted to order a dry martini with an olive in a chilled glass," Louis says. "We were almost thrown in jail."

"What if he doesn't know how to make a Sea Breeze?" I ask Louis. "What if he's also"—I motion around the room—"a demented hillbilly?"

"So we're not at Roxbury. Lighten up," Louis says. "So the place doesn't have a VIP room. *Never* let trouble with a woman do this to you. Relax."

"I quit *Sun City*," I say.

Louis taps his fingers on the bar. "What do you mean? I thought you were almost done."

"I don't want to do it anymore."

Locals come inside, head for the pool table. Girls by a video game stare at me.

The bartender puts up the drinks. Louis tastes his and gives the bartender thumbs-up.

"Four dollars," the bartender says, unimpressed.

Louis gulps his drink, finishes it. "This one's on my boy Emery."

I hand the man some money.

At the jukebox Louis puts in quarters and selects "Born to Run" six separate times, nudges me, raising his eyebrows. "Irony, huh?" Louis takes my drink and sips. "So what are they doing? Without their lead man they're fucked."

One of the girls by the video games starts to walk over.

"Relax," Louis says. "Everyone's having a good time. Look, you got your jukebox here, pool table, friendly bartender. I know you'd rather be hanging out with Bruce and Demi at The Ivy, but *relax*. This place is great."

The girl taps me on the shoulder.

"You're Emery Roberts," the girl says, turning back to her friends for a second, smiling.

"No, *I'm* Emery Roberts," Louis says.

The girl doesn't look at Louis. "Um, I just wanted to say hi. And I really liked you in *Top Gun*."

I nod, even though I wasn't in *Top Gun*.

"No, I'm Emery Roberts," Louis says, bowing. "And I'm delighted by the compliment."

The girl goes back to her friends. One of them squeals.

I drain half the Sea Breeze, dizzy.

Louis leers at them, thumps his fist on his other palm. "Creatures," he whispers.

"Creatures," I say.

He thumps his fist again, grins, and winks. *"Local* creatures."

"You have a girlfriend," I say. "Or is that plural?"

"Who's Plural?" Louis asks, blinking. "I never had a creature named Plural."

Louis waves to the girls, doesn't look at me. "My boy Emery doesn't seem to understand that if you don't appreciate *other* creatures, you can't appreciate your *own*."

I glance over at the girls. They giggle; one of them squeals again.

"America loves him and he wants to quit," Louis says, finishing my drink. "Oboy."

We sit with Anne and Danny. Danny has the camera going, interviewing Anne.

"Why do you think he did it?" Danny asks her.

"Maybe you should ask him yourself." Anne yawns.

Danny points the camera at me. "Well?" Danny asks. "Why?"

"Why what, Danny?" Louis asks good-naturedly.

"Why did Emery effectively shut down a forty-million-dollar production?"

"Without Emery," Anne points out, "there *is* no production. Bet Monty's popping a vein. Unless of course, they try to shoot around this, uh, problem."

"The second unit can only shoot so many cars exploding," Louis murmurs gravely. "The creature's got a point."

I look at my hands.

"You're going to get sued," Anne mumbles, drunk. "My father'll be the first in line."

"Fuck sued," Louis mutters. "We need more drinks. We need Sea Breeze."

Jeremiah and Nathan walk in and come over to our table.

"Jeremiah filled me in," Nathan says, unsmiling. "I think it's hilarious. If somehow I don't get my production bonus on this one, you and I are going to fistfight."

"How are you going to fight with something that's not technically . . . here?" Jeremiah asks.

"Interesting dilemma," Danny says.

Concerned, Anne taps me on the shoulder. "Emery. They're insulting you. Do you understand, Emery?"

"I don't know," I say.

Nathan moves over to the video games.

Jeremiah sits down.

"My boy Nathan's making a swimming pool," Louis says. "Unfortunately it's with his bare hands, but he's sure that the final product will be a pool nonetheless."

"Didn't anyone tell him there's a lake on your property?" Danny asks. "Or like, what's the situation?"

Anne stares at me sadly. "I was just telling Emery that Monty's going to pop a vein when he finds out."

Another song comes on the jukebox, not "Born to Run." Danny lights a cigarette.

"Who cares?" Jeremiah says, waving away the smoke.

Louis hands me a hundred-dollar bill. "Drinks! A round for the house in celebration of Emery's arrival. The newest Hollywood refugee."

At the bar Anne asks, "Does this mean you're available for dating?" She closes her eyes, reeking of bourbon. "You asshole."

I hand the bartender the hundred-dollar bill.

"My friend wants to buy everyone here a round of drinks," I say.

The bartender nods. "What's his name?"

I wake up late, take a shower, go downstairs. All of the doorknobs in this house are missing. It's one, maybe two in the afternoon, and I'm in the kitchen. There are sprout and tahini sandwiches on the table. A black woman, maybe my agent's age, peels jicama.

"Gladys," she says, nods to the sandwiches. "Hungry?"

I pick one up and smell it.

"Do you know where everyone is?" I ask, my voice cracking, dry.

"Lake," she says.

"Seen a guy with a camera?"

She starts to laugh, then shakes her head. "I saw him. Just twenty minutes ago. He slept late, too."

"Is he there?" I say. "I mean, at the lake?"

She laughs out loud. "Said he was going swimming."

I stare at her for a while. "That's . . . good. It's really hot here. I mean, right?"

She keeps laughing, peeling jicama.

I look at my sandwich.

"He *thinks* he's going swimming, but that lake's full of turtles. Biting turtles. I said to him, 'Why do you suppose they call it Turtle Lake?' and he said, 'Probably because it's shaped like a turtle.' That one isn't so bright, I guess."

I look at the sandwich before saying, "No."

"Turtle Lake. No one goes swimming there. There's a rowboat, about as close to that water as you can get." Gladys laughs again. " 'Is it shaped like a turtle?' he said. No, that camera boy's a dummy."

I finish the sandwich, take a few beers from the fridge. They are still attached to the plastic six-pack thing.

"Which way is it?" I ask.

"Path at the back of the house. Only leads one place."

Gladys laughs again, this time hard, then wipes tears from her eyes with the hand holding the peeler.

"That one boy Nathan got bit last week. That one's a dummy, too, I suppose. Taken to digging his own swimming pool, so's there's nothing to bite him. Trying to finish it by the end of the summer, the boy's got himself a race I don't think he's going to win." Gladys stops laughing. "It's not so easy to take care of a houseful of dummies."

I look out at the hills, finding it hard to breathe. I slap at a mosquito and miss.

"You're in the movies, right? I've seen you in the movies. That one about the spies."

"That was me," I say.

I pass by the hole in the backyard and start up the narrow path for Turtle Lake.

I walk maybe five minutes. There Louis is juggling three turtles, humming circus music. Danny has the camera turned on Anne, interviewing her. Jeremiah sits with a screwdriver, fixing and polishing the missing doorknobs from the house.

Louis asks, "Is that beer you have there?"

Louis stops juggling the turtles, catches them, then throws them back in the water. He takes a beer, and we watch the turtle shells sinking, the animals coming out of their shells, swimming away.

A radio plays somewhere. Danny, done with Anne, now points the camera out over the water.

"Your houseboy Danny got bit," Louis says.

"Where?" I ask. "By who?"

"On the leg," Louis says. "In the lake. On the leg."

A loud popping sound echoes out over the lake.

Louis interrupts. "Nathan's losing it."

Out across the water, where Danny is pointing the camera, a small rowboat floats in the middle of the lake. Nathan stands in it, a rifle aimed at the water. The gun goes off again; a popping sound echoes.

"Nathan," Jeremiah yells. "Be careful."

Nathan waves absentmindedly with a free hand. Danny walks over, camera pointed at me.

"Nathan's hunting turtles," Louis says. "He got bit five days ago. Nathan's a little pissed off."

Nathan stands up again in the boat. He hits the water with an oar, then starts to row.

"Over here," Louis yells.

Nathan guides the boat to where we stand. Danny videotapes it.

" 'Over here?' Where the fuck else would I go, you moron?" Nathan snaps.

"Hey, you're the one who wrote Mickey Rourke's last movie," Louis snaps back.

"Yeah, but he turned down the assignment on *Weekend at Bernie's II,*" Danny says. "You gotta respect that."

"What did you do?" Anne asks Danny. "When you were bitten."

"Smoked a joint," Louis says.

Danny, from behind the camera, silently gives us thumbs-up, continues taping.

Louis points to Anne adjusting her bathing suit, sitting on a big white towel.

"Anne's always been one of the finer creatures," Louis says admiringly.

"Creature," Anne says, unamused. "Makes me feel lovely. Wanted."

Louis thumps his fist against his palm. "Creature."

Danny repeats the gesture, a little unsure. "Creature," Danny says.

Nathan staggers out of the rowboat and hands me the rifle as he walks onshore. I look into the barrel: a BB gun. Danny has the camera pointed straight at my face. I aim the gun at the lens, but he doesn't move. I aim it at my head, but Danny turns the camera on Louis, who blows him a kiss.

"Disgusting faggot," Nathan mutters.

"On the record?" Louis says. "Louis *es no* bisexual. Strictly creatures with big tits for this boy."

"Does that rule out Arnold Schwarzenegger?" Danny asks.

"You can see we have a problem here," Nathan says, taking back the gun.

"Yeah," Louis says. "A shitty screenwriter thinks I'm a raving fag."

"Shitty screenwriter who's got a hell of a lot more money than—what are you again? Out-of-work agent, is it?" Nathan scans the surface of the lake. "How sad."

"Nathan got bitten, too," Danny says.

Nathan holds up one finger. "Only once."

Louis forces a giggle and puts his arm around Nathan's shoulder. "Nathan's angry. That's why he's building his own animal-free swimming hole. Going to get some revenge, aren't you, Nathan?"

Nathan looks dead serious. "Want to go out there?" he asks me. "They're thickest around the center of the pond."

"I thought this was a . . . lake," I say. "Right?"

Louis shrugs.

"They swim in *packs*," Nathan says, eyes wide.

"I believe the correct term is *gaggles*. Schools of fish, herds of buffalo, *gaggles* of turtles," Anne says, eyes closed, tying her hair into a knot. "I could really use a line."

"Another all-day drunkathon, my little baby?" Jeremiah doesn't look up from a knob he polishes.

Danny tapes Nathan and Louis and me as we get into the boat and push off from shore, then speaks, like a narrator from a nature show.

"And so, another generation goes out to sea, and the old shall teach the young, as they have done for centuries, how to hunt, and survive, in the wild and new wilderness . . ."

Louis rows out to the middle of the lake, finding Nathan's exact spot. Danny opens beer, and I lie on my back on one of the seats. It's quiet for a couple of minutes, just the sound of water lapping against the side of the metal boat.

Nathan stands up, moves around. I open my eyes and grab the side of the hull. Nathan is pointing the gun at the water. "There!"

"You're not going to hit any of them," Louis says. "Why don't you just relax, dude? Soak up the sun."

Nathan says nothing, pumps the gun twice.

Louis is resting his hand over the side of the boat, absent-mindedly twirling his fingers in the water. "What have you got against turtles?"

"See this?" Nathan shows us the marks on his leg. "They tried to eat me. I was just swimming here. I was just minding my own business and they attacked me and tried to kill me."

Water moves all around us in the lake, little ripples, the constant motion of its surface. Onshore Danny interviews Jeremiah, while Anne sleeps.

"I don't think they like the fact that we took over," Louis says, opening another beer. "No one lived in this house for fifty years before Jeremiah bought it. We're intruding on their space. Ask Emery."

"Ask Emery? I'd get a more detailed response from a lemon," Nathan says, keeping his aim on the water. "Besides, turtles are just like that. Real territorial."

Louis swirls his hand in the lake, sprinkles some water on his legs. "Turtletorial."

Nathan puts the gun down and sits, shaking his head miserably. "I wish Jeremiah kept a real gun."

"Nathan," Louis says. "Nathan, I said you're invading their territory. They're protective. They'll try to *force* you out. They'll try to eat you."

"I'm listening to someone whose biggest client was one of the 'Uh-Huh' girls," Nathan says. "Before she dumped him."

I finish my beer.

Nathan spots something move in the water, raises the gun, squints as he aims and fires. The BBs hit the surface and splash.

"Shit," Nathan says. "I need a more powerful weapon."

Anne gets up and yells from shore, "Did you get one?"

Nathan shakes his head, waves Anne away, dismissing her.

Louis's eyes open wide, his face red with pain. He pulls his hand out of the water. A finger is bleeding.

"Shit," Louis says, sucking his finger.

"See?" Nathan says. "See what I mean?"

"Maybe you can buy some explosives or something, you big handsome hunter you." Louis blows him a kiss.

Louis hears that in New York State one can drink until four in the morning. After last call at the D, we drive across the state line to a place called Moshi Moshi Honky Tonk Sushi.

Anne and I shoot pool and Louis and Nathan order double sakes, pick bad songs on the jukebox, sing along with them. Danny sits across a table from Jeremiah, camera going. Jeremiah makes faces. Louis and Nathan finally sit down at the table with Jeremiah and Danny. The camera is pointed at Nathan now, who talks to it, serious look on his face. There is a Japanese man in a cowboy hat behind the bar. Everyone is getting drunk.

"Nathan's talking about turtles." Anne leans over to take a shot and I can sort of see down her shirt. She misses, looks a little disappointed. "A screenwriter will do anything not to write."

Young girls walk in and the bartender asks for ID. Predictably they spot someone, recognize me. One of the girls gets a beer, licks the neck of the bottle, showing tongue, tries to look me in the eye, then walks past me out the door.

I feel a hand on my shoulder.

Louis says, "See the way she looked at me?"

"How's Becky?" Anne asks. "How's Becky, Louis?"

"Are you trying to ruin my fun?" Louis asks.

"I'll tell her," Anne warns. "Besides. *This* is fun?"

"That girl gave me a sign," Louis says. "She wants me. The creature *wants* her prey." He thumps his fist against the palm of his hand, and he walks out the door, following the girl.

Anne doesn't want to play anymore and I've lost track of the game. She sits on a stool and watches me try a trick shot. It doesn't work.

"Are any supposed to sink, Emery?" she asks.

"Sorry," Jeremiah says, coming up behind me. "I saw it on ESPN. Minnesota Fats did it. He does them all."

"What's Nathan talking about over there?" Anne says. "I'm not really interested, but Emery's dazzling conversational skills seem misplaced tonight, and I'm starved for some smart talk."

"What do you *think?*" Jeremiah hands me a glass full of pink liquid. "Sea Breeze, right?"

I take a sip and try the shot again. Nothing sinks.

Jeremiah puts his arm around Anne and kisses her head. "My sister beat you? She's good at pool."

"Actually, very big brother," Anne says, "I'm not even good at that."

Louis bangs on the window from outside, sticks his tongue out, thumps his fist. The girl looks in also, waves.

"That poor girl," Anne murmurs.

"That poor girl gets what she deserves," Jeremiah says.

"No one deserves to get date-raped by a talking beer keg." Anne sighs.

Danny comes over to the pool table and kneels so that the camera is level with the felt.

"Get away," Jeremiah says. "Very tricky shot here."

Danny points the camera at Jeremiah's face and Jeremiah almost raises the cue stick like a baseball bat. Danny continues taping, doesn't flinch.

"You can't do much about him, can you?" Anne asks someone.

Jeremiah shakes his head. "USC film students. Always ill behaved."

I take a shot, nothing sinks. The girl from outside looks in the window again, at me, beer in hand. Louis comes up behind her, smells her hair. She yelps, laughs.

"Maybe I should go get Louis," Anne says. "Save this poor girl."

Anne walks outside, and Danny moves around the room with the camera, annoying drunken locals. Jeremiah takes a few shots.

"You bored yet?" Jeremiah asks me.

"Not really," I say. "I mean, what's 'bored'?"

"Wait until you've been here two weeks. That's usually the turning point for people who live in cities."

"Two weeks," I say, lighting a cigarette.

Jeremiah takes a shot. "Does anyone know where you are? Or are you in hiding?"

"Sort of," I mumble.

"Anne's right. My father is going to lose it."

I shrug. "Sorry?"

"Doesn't matter," Jeremiah says, concentrating on the table. "I could give a shit about that whole business."

"Are you going to live up here?" I ask. "Forever?"

Jeremiah picks up the cue ball and looks at it. "I'm sort

of running out of money. And once my father finds out that I'm housing you, we won't speak for a year or two, so hitting him up is out of the question."

"Monty won't find out," I say. "No one has to know."

"He'll find you," Jeremiah says. "They always find you. What do you know about wood floors?"

"They're wooden," I say, then after a pause: "I think."

"Having a little existential crisis, are we?" Jeremiah asks. "I think I should tell you it's been done before."

The pay phone is at the back of the restaurant, and I call Danielle's number in L.A. There is static over the line.

"Where are you?" Danielle, illusion of calmness.

"At a Japanese place."

"Are you drinking?" I hear Danielle ask. "Are you drunk?"

"Yes."

"Tell me where you are. I'll come pick you up. Don't drive."

"There's little chance of that," I say.

"Why didn't you call before?"

"I'm calling now."

"Where are you, Emery?"

"I can only tell you this. I'm a couple of time zones away."

"You're in Japan. I knew it," she hisses. "Damnit."

"I'm in a Japanese restaurant," I say. "Relax."

"Katsu? Matsuhisa? Where?" Danielle asks.

"Oh, shit, Danielle." I sigh, hand covering my eyes.

Silence over the line. Music from the jukebox makes it hard to hear.

"People are looking for you. You're going to miss your call tomorrow."

I can hear her laughing.

"Maybe you should just fly back. From wherever it is you are. I'll stall Monty for a couple of days. I'll say you went on a bender. I'll say great actors are like that. He'll probably believe me."

I listen to the static. Everything spins, slowly. "I'm not coming back."

"This is your career we're talking about here. This isn't some two-hundred-grand-a-year-I-had-a-series-for-two-years career. I'm talking about a *gift*."

"Please," I say. "Really."

"The picture's going to shut down, baby," Danielle says. "They'll sue you. You'll lose credibility."

I look at my hand, my wrist.

"Are you there?"

I can hear someone else's conversation on the line, muffled, bits and pieces of it.

"Too late," I say.

"Why are you doing this?" She's crying.

"What do you want me to do?"

"Come back. If not for the stupid picture, then for me."

"We talked about that," I say.

"You can't walk from a job this big," Danielle says. "You can't walk from a lead opposite Hurley. You can't just walk out after twelve weeks of shooting."

"Jeremiah said I get more money than him."

A long pause.

"Are you up there?" Danielle asks.

I look around. Danny has the camera pointed at me. "No."

"You can't just walk out. And not tell anyone why or anything."

"I don't want to do it anymore."

"What the fuck are you talking about?"

"I have to go."

I hang up.

"Drama," Danny says, putting the camera at his side. "That was great stuff there, Emery. I especially liked the 'us isn't still us' part. Great stuff. You're a genius talent."

I walk outside. Louis sits between Anne and the girl. The girl stares at me, smiles.

"Emery Roberts," Louis says. "This is Mona. Mona, Emery Roberts."

Mona gets up and shakes my hand, kisses me on the cheek.

"Mona is *very* friendly," Anne says.

Mona maybe doesn't hear Anne and sits back down next to Louis, who puts his arms around the two girls.

"Emery," Louis says. "I've got two, count 'em, two women here. I have full creature potential."

"He's got *no* creature potential," Anne says, standing up and taking my hand.

Louis moves closer to Mona and sniffs strands of her hair.

"Louis has a girlfriend," Anne says to Mona.

"She's lying," Louis says. "Anne wants me to herself."

"I'd rather have Epstein-Barr," Anne says.

"Do you have a girlfriend?" Mona asks me. "I mean, up here?"

"It's just that they smell so good," Louis says. "It gets us under their spell."

"Is he always this way?" Mona asks.

"Yes." Anne nods. "He has a hormone imbalance. And at any given time of the month, a massive case of crabs."

"What about you, Emery?" Mona asks.

Anne puts her arms around me. "Spoken for."

"Oh," Mona says, turning to Louis. "I'm going back inside."

Louis flashes me a hateful look and follows Mona inside. Anne leans on the hood of Louis's car.

"Thanks for saving me," I say, sarcastic.

"If I was capable of saving you," she says, "I would have done that a long time ago."

The music from inside is muffled, loud.

Mona runs out of the bar, laughing. She hands me a piece of paper.

"My phone number," Mona says, without looking at Anne. "Call whenever."

"Tomorrow you have an eight o'clock call," Anne says after Mona leaves with Louis. "What are the odds you'll make it?"

"What are the odds that you think I'll make it?"

"What are the odds that I care?"

Upstairs I pass an open door. Inside is what used to be a bathroom, now completely gutted. There are pipes sticking out of the walls and in the corner is a toilet sitting on its side. Jeremiah wrestles with a pipe and wrench, his back turned toward me. His shirt is off, and he sweats and grunts, muscles red and swollen, trying to loosen something. He doesn't see me. I don't say anything.

After a long, hard pull on the wrench, a pipe breaks and a gush of water knocks him down, soaking him. Jeremiah doesn't get out of the way of the rushing water. Instead he sits there, hitting the wrench on the floor. Water is everywhere. I walk down the hall.

At the end of the hall is a door, painted red. There isn't much in this room: white walls, some plaster missing, no furniture, someone's ghetto blaster sits in the corner, tapes, a jar full of colored pens, cans of paint, empty CD boxes. On the far wall someone has painted in big blue letters:

WALL

I put on some music, U2, and sit on the floor, light a cigarette and watch the smoke float in humid air. Laughing outside, then Louis's laugh, unmistakable it's so loud. Later in the afternoon I crawl over to the jar and take out some pens, draw on the wall. A smileyface in green, then sunglasses for it, in red. Bright light comes through the windows and mosquitoes are everywhere.

I walk in circles around the hole in the backyard while Danny points the camera.

"Emery," Danny says. "I guess you missed your call."

"Danny."

"I guess you feel pretty bad, huh?"

"I'm supposed to help Nathan today."

Danny says, "Uh, is that your excuse?"

Nathan comes up the path from the lake.

"What's going on?" Danny asks.

"Fucking turtles is what's going on," Nathan says. "Do you have a cigarette?"

Danny hands him one and a pack of matches from Chinois.

"No way to get rid of them?" Danny asks.

"Mothers are everywhere." Nathan lights the cigarette and speaks with it hanging from his lips. He points at the hole. "That's why we've got to get that thing finished."

The hole is maybe the size of a shallow grave with a pile of dirt next to it. "The pool. How long do you think it'll take?" Danny asks.

"I don't know," Nathan says. "Never built one. Of course, it would be faster if I had a backhoe or something, but I kind of like doing it by hand."

"What about cement?" Danny asks. "Cement for the walls and sides."

"We'll get to that when we get to that," Nathan snaps. "We can't get it done too soon, though, if you ask me. It's so fucking hot and sticky here."

"Weren't you writing a screenplay?" Danny asks.

"I can't do anything if I have to live in this goddamn heat. I need water. I need a body of water where I won't get chewed on by some animal."

"Well that rules out Kim Basinger's Jacuzzi," Danny says.

"You're like some kind of goat," Nathan says, staring at Danny. "Like some kind of goat with an expensive camcorder."

Nathan starts to walk away.

"Don't take it so hard," Danny says. "We'll get it done."

"We have to." Nathan keeps walking. "If we don't get it done, if we can't swim even just one time by the end of this summer, just fucking once in the pool, it means we *lose*. Turtles win, we *lose*. That simple."

We head back to the house, and Danny follows us, the camera going.

Nathan stops, looks into the lens. Danny zooms in a little.

"I've tried shooting them with the BB gun," Nathan says, sadly, slowly as if he's confused by something. "But that doesn't seem to be doing much of anything. I hit a couple with an oar and knocked them out and captured them, until they . . . regained consciousness . . . and escaped . . . But I estimate their numbers in the hundreds, possibly thousands."

"So you're saying the problem is too big?" Danny zooms in more. "What can we, the ordinary Hollywood refugee, do?"

"You can help make this pool," Nathan says. "I mean it. I'm playing with the idea of a net at the lake, but in the meantime, we need help with the swimming pool. Everyone seems to have better things to do, though. I'm the only one so far who wants to swim bad enough to do anything about it."

Nathan walks away, mumbling something to himself.

Danny turns off the camera and waves a joint in front of my face. We sit over by the side of the house and smoke the whole thing. After a while I see everything in a different way. Louis's car pulls up and Anne and Louis get out, come over, sit down. No one says a word. Louis winks and I try to smile. It's cooler out, but not much. Four of us stare at the sunset even though two of us aren't stoned.

We are lost. In the middle of nowhere. Louis is drunker than anyone and driving home.

"Wait a minute," Louis says. "I recognize that. I recognize that sign. Todd Hill Road. Okay, I know where we are. Todd Hill."

"Todd Hill," Anne yells drunkenly. "Todd Hill. Make a—make a left. Right. I mean, right. Right turn."

"What?" Louis asks.

"What the hell are you doing?" Anne screams.

"Shut up," Louis says. "Just lower your fucking voice, bitch."

"You're a fucker, you know that?" Anne says. She leans her head against my shoulder. "He's a fucking fucker. Louis is a fucker."

"I know where we're going. We're going this way. I know where we're going," Louis says. He turns around and smiles, then mouths "bitch."

"Eyes on the road," Anne says. "You retarded asshole."

"I know where we're going." Louis turns back to face the road. "My boy Emery doesn't trust me?"

"Why should we trust *you?*" Anne says. "We've been lost out here for an hour."

Anne's hand slips up my thigh as she tries to steady herself to look out the window. I doubt she can really see anything anyway. At this moment it doesn't seem like there is anyone, anywhere, that isn't the way we are.

"I have to piss," Danny groans from the front seat.

"I know where we are," Louis says. "We're almost there."

"I have to piss right *now,*" Danny says.

"Emery," Anne says. "Your entourage up there needs to piss."

"Why don't you just open your mouth, Anne, so we won't have to stop?" Louis suggests.

"Emery," Anne says. "*Do* something."

Louis pulls over, next to a fence. I look out the window. I think I can see cows.

"Emery's entourage has to piss." Louis sighs. "Let him piss. There's a hierarchy here. Even in Vermont. I'm accommodating myself to it."

We get out of the Saab. Danny stumbles into the bushes. Anne sits on the hood of the car, looks at the sky.

"Shooting star," she says.

Louis looks up.

"Missed it," Anne says.

"It was an airplane," Louis says.

I stand in the yard watching Nathan dig. It's eleven, maybe midnight and Nathan has been at it for hours. It doesn't seem like any progress has been made.

I go over to the back steps and sit there, tired, looking out at the trees, fireflies. Mosquitoes buzz around my ears. I slap at my neck every couple of seconds. Anne opens the door, holding a half-read screenplay.

"Half of Hollywood is probably looking for you today." Anne leans her face into my shoulder and mumbles into my sleeve. "You should go to bed."

Her hand reaches into my shirt, touches a nipple, lightly.

Inside, at the bottom of the stairs, Anne stops. "You first. I need inspiration."

She kisses my neck, unbuttons my shirt, and I'm standing there, even though I'd rather sleep, letting her.

Anne pours herself more wine and leans against my legs, absentmindedly touching one of my feet.

Jeremiah walks in. "I'm cutting off the electricity."

Anne looks irritated. "Emery and I are watching this."

"Why don't you watch the news?" Jeremiah asks. "Why the hell is this game show so interesting to you? Emery's way of studying for his high school equivalency test?"

"Jeremiah's getting indignant." Anne sighs. "Jesus. It's only 'Jeopardy!' "

"I'm cutting the power," Jeremiah says.

"Don't turn off the electricity," Anne says. "Do *not* turn off the electricity."

"Watch 'This Old House,' " Jeremiah says. "I think they're going to do wood floors today."

"Emery?" Anne asks, distracted. "Wood floors?"

"I don't care what we watch," I say. "I have no opinion."

"Centrifugal force," Anne mutters.

One of the contestants is being told that he got the question wrong. The question they were looking for was "What is centrifugal force?"

"Why do they make you answer in questions?" Anne asks. "Why the fuck do they make people do that?"

"Don't do it, Emery," Jeremiah says. "I'm king here, remember?"

I blow out the match, toss the unlit cigarette on the table.

"I'm going to turn the electricity off," Jeremiah says. *"Five* minutes."

Jeremiah walks out of the room.

Anne changes the channel and throws the remote over to me.

"Watch whatever you want," Anne says. "I don't care."

There is a girl on the screen who once did a small part in a high school movie I did. She is flying through the air now, holding a hamburger, looking at it like she's in love with it. This is followed by a Starburst commercial.

"Jesus, it's *hot.*" Anne stands up, ruffles the front of her T-shirt. It sort of sticks to her and she isn't wearing a bra. I look back at the TV.

"I'm going into the kitchen for some ice," Anne says.

I flip through channels, stop at the news. People are protesting in front of a big building. I change the channel. My name appears on the screen in block letters, then Hurley Thompson's, then *Sun City*. An advance preview, a montage of footage that was shot early on; in the corner of the screen is the "Entertainment Tonight" logo, *"Sun City,"* the announcer says. "This Christmas. Feel the heat." This is followed by Mary Hart's chirping voice.

I hit the mute button and change the channel. A Bob Hope movie is on. I change the channel. For a second I see my face, laughing, from a movie I did about football. I change the channel back to "Jeopardy!"

Anne walks in and hands me a new beer. I take a sip from the new one, the old one still half full in my other hand.

"What do you want to do?" Anne looks at me.

I shrug.

"We'll take you into town. After Final Jeopardy," Anne says. "Is that an acceptable suggestion?"

Louis comes in, takes one of my beers, and sits on the floor.

"Is it cool to take this?" Louis asks, sipping.

Anne holds ice between her fingers, letting drops fall on my leg.

"I've returned from the lake," Louis says, staring at the TV, concentrating.

Anne leans over and puts a small piece of ice down the front of my shorts. I can't feel it, so I leave it there.

"Can we use your car to go into town?" Anne asks Louis.

Louis turns around. "What? I can't go?"

"No, you can't go," she says. "But did I say you couldn't go?"

I stare at my hands, back and front.

"I'll go." Louis shrugs. "I'll go wherever the fuck I want to."

"We should get all of Emery's movies at the Video Palace," Anne says. "Don't you think that would be fun?" Anne pauses. "Or at least mean?"

"Let's get all of Monty's movies instead," Louis says. "Let's rent *Invisible Cop*, *Invisible Cop 2*, *Blood on the Cop*, *Shrimp Weaver*. The list goes on and on."

"I've seen all of Monty's movies a million times," Anne groans, rolling her eyes. "*Invisible Cop 2*, maybe more than a million."

"His films cover the entire spectrum of cinematic imbecility," Louis says. "Remember *Woof?* About the singing Jack Russell terrier? Wasn't Emery in that one?"

"Emery was in the one about the talking car," Anne says, staring at the TV. *"Vroom*, it was called. Emery got second billing. Under the car."

Louis says to the TV, "What is Maui?"

One of the contestants says, "What is Molokai?" and Alex Trebek says, "Right. You have control of the board. Pick a category."

"Shit," Louis says.

Anne gets up. "Louis, we need the keys to your car."

Louis finishes his beer, shudders. "I'm going with. Besides, I have to go to the state liquor store. Can you imagine having the government control all the alcohol?"

"But what if I don't want a raving asshole to drive me?" Anne asks sweetly.

"What if I don't want someone who barely survives alcohol poisoning on a daily basis in the car with *me*?" Louis asks, then adds, "Jesus, can you imagine the shits this bitch must take every morning?"

"I can't listen to this," I say.

Louis pats my leg. "We're going to rent all of your movies? Your entire illustrious career right before our eyes?"

Louis lights a cigarette as we pull out of the driveway onto the road. I sit in front, Anne in the backseat, sitting all the way forward between me and Louis, her hand rubbing my shoulder, hard. I try to move so she'll stop, but she doesn't.

"What's 'can' backwards?" Anne asks after a little while.

"What?" Louis says.

"What's 'can' backwards? How do you say 'can' backwards?"

"Nack." Louis sighs.

"Right. What's 'book' backwards?"

"Koob." Louis sighs again.

"What's 'Emery' backwards?" Anne asks.

"Yaremma," Louis says. "Yameree."

"What's 'paper' backwards?"

"Repap," Louis answers. "Anne, hand over that flask of joy juice. Before you *really* lose it."

"What's 'chicken' backwards?" Anne asks.

Louis is not looking at the road. He tries to find the right song on the tape deck.

"Nickitch," Louis says. "Emery, ask Anne if she is willing to change the topic of conversation."

"Close. What's 'tomboy' backwards?"

"Yobmot."

"What's 'yam' backwards?"

"What?" Louis says. "You're crazy. You're a crazy bitch who comes from a crazy family."

"What's 'dog' backwards?" Anne asks.

"God," Louis mutters. "Certifiable."

"What's 'Marlboro' backwards?"

"Orolbram?" Louis says.

"Oroblram. What's 'food' backwards?"

"Doof," Louis says, grinning. "Doof, doof, doof."

Louis feeds the car gas, making screeching tire sounds.

"What's 'sympathize' backwards?" Anne asks.

Louis is giggling. "Emery, oh God, please help her."

" 'Sympathize' backwards?" Anne asks again, an edge in her voice.

"Esithapims," Louis says.

"Close enough," Anne says. "What's 'boyfriend' backwards?"

Louis swerves to miss a dog.

"Daneerfyob," Louis says. "Boyfriend is daneerfyob, Anne. And I'm beginning to realize why you don't have one."

"Right," Anne says, giving my shoulder a squeeze. "What's 'sex' backwards?"

"Xes."

"What's 'racecar' backwards?" Anne asks.

Sitting on my bed with a pen and a piece of paper, I can't remember the last time I wrote a letter to anyone. I am hoping this will be one of those letters that will tie things up nicely.

I stare at the blank page, sometimes doodling or writing Danielle's name in the center. I try to draw a picture of the house, Nathan's swimming pool, the Concorde, caricatures of Hurley Thompson, Keanu, Jason, Luke, Donovan, Flea, the rest of them.

A knock at the door. Louis comes in with beer.

I look around the room, lights on, at myself, fully clothed.

"I'm sleeping," I say, suddenly very tired.

Louis sits on an unopened suitcase, checks his watch.

"It is now three-thirty," Louis says. "Middle of the night. Dead calm middle and my boy Emery's still up."

I look at the mangled tip of my pen, where I've been chewing on it.

"Writing?" Louis asks.

"Trying."

"A letter?" Louis laughs. "Why don't you use the phone?"

"I know," I say. "I don't even know how to write one."

"I just called Becky," Louis says, gulping beer.

"Did you tell Becky I was here?" I ask.

Louis shakes his head. "If they find you, it's not going to be because of me. Fuck that. I know what you're doing. I'm doing the same thing, sort of."

"What did Becky say?" I ask.

" 'No one hires gorillas to break Emery Roberts's legs,' " Louis says.

"I'm costing people a lot of money," I say. "Did Becky say that?"

"Do you give a shit?" Louis asks. "No. Are they ever going to find you? No."

"What else did Becky say?"

"What do you know about Briston Folkes?" Louis asks. "Besides *not* being on the Ten Sexiest Men Alive list this year?"

"Very little," I murmur, realizing that I was on that list.

"Did you ever see him hitting on Becky?" Louis asks. "Not Briston the director, Briston Jr., the son. Briston Jr. the prick. The drug addict. The scumbag with film all over him."

"Briston's probably . . ." I start, "a . . . very nice guy."

"I called and got Becky's machine," Louis says. "I know the code, so I checked her messages."

A long pause. Louis tears at the label on the bottle.

"Anything interesting?" I ask.

"Someone called to say something about *Sun City*. About there being an indefinite *hiatus* from shooting."

I mumble something about a body double.

"And then there was a message from little Briston. He said something like 'Becky, baby, this is Briston Jr. calling. I know it's late, but I'm at the Olive and—"

"What about you and the town girls?"

Louis doesn't even pause. "Different situation. Becky's going to Briston's house because Becky's ambitious. Because the creature gets off on big names. Star fuckers, everyone's a star fucker."

I nod.

"You can't get any starrier than you. Who the hell could you want to fuck, bigger than you? Madonna maybe?"

"Maybe," I say, yawning. "I don't know."

"Fuck Becky," Louis says. "Becky uses herself, lets everyone use her, and all she cares about is the check."

"Dating an actress . . ." I mumble.

Louis finishes his beer and takes mine, starts drinking. I crumple the piece of paper I was drawing on, light a cigarette.

"Jeremiah'll kill you. Radical ex-smokers. Borderline psychotics."

"If anyone calls, I'm not here," I say, trying to phrase this as carefully as possible. "You haven't seen me."

The backyard. The afternoon sun is very hot. Nathan works in silence for a long time, digging, throwing shovelfuls of dirt on the pile next to the hole, which by now is the size of two graves, side by side. He stops to wipe sweat from his forehead, then to take off his T-shirt. A whistle from the house. Anne is in a window on the second floor. Danny sticks his head out the window, too, camera going, pointed down at us. I flex my arm muscles and Danny puts down the camera.

"Disgusting Emery," Danny says. His head disappears again.

Anne yells down. "We're in your room. We're going through your things, hot stuff." Her head disappears inside.

"Doesn't that bother you?" Nathan asks.

I shake my head. "What's left?"

"People with girlfriends and boyfriends tend to get non-productive. They spend a lot of 'quality time' together; they dawdle. They learn how to make cappuccino; they join AA; they rent *Dances with Wolves* and cry together when Two Socks dies. Now that you're not used as an actor anymore, you can spend more time on the job at hand. This pool can be your girlfriend." Nathan pauses. "It's mine."

He resumes shoveling, and the dog runs up, sniffs at us, then runs away.

"That dog's name is Kevin," Nathan says. "That is not a good dog name."

"I'm getting something to drink," I say. "From inside."

"Why don't you use the hose?" Nathan suggests. "Faster that way."

Nathan looks at me funny. I go to the side of the house and drink from the hose. The water tastes thick, hot, not like water. I go back to the hole and watch Nathan digging.

"This is good for me," Nathan says. "It relaxes me not to think about the *business.*"

"Well, that's why you're doing this here," I say, slowly, pointing to the hole. "I mean . . . right?"

Anne opens the back door, goes to the hose, and turns it on, wetting her hair, her head, back, water pouring all over her.

Finally, dripping, she says, "Any minute. Any minute, Emery. The hammer's going to fall."

Danny carries my black leather suitcases downstairs and sets them next to the front door. He then tears up a few cardboard boxes to make signs. I don't think the house has an address, so the signs have arrows, and GARAGE SALE TODAY scrawled on them.

Danny's now in the front room, playing with the video camera, mumbling something to himself.

"You'll drive me?" I ask.

"Drive yourself." Danny throws me his keys. I don't catch them.

"I don't know how," I say. "To drive."

"You're useless. Where?" Danny points the camera at my face. "Around here? Around town?"

"I guess."

Danny gathers the signs and borrows a hammer and nails from Jeremiah. When we pull onto the road, Danny says, "Steer." He lets go of the wheel, expecting me to grab it.

"I don't want to steer," I say, taking it.

He takes his camera from the backseat and points it straight ahead, at where we're going.

"Is this legal?" I ask.

"As if you care, Emery," Danny says, turning the camera to the right, aiming at my face. "As if that's ever stopped you before."

I say, "I'm letting go."

"Your funeral," Danny says, the camera pointed ahead of us again. "But hey, good career move."

I let go of the steering wheel and Danny turns off the camera, puts it in the backseat. He reaches over to the glove compartment and pulls out a plastic bag, pot, some joints already rolled.

"Smoke or something," Danny says. "You're tense."

"It's nine in the morning," I say.

Danny reaches into the bag, lights a joint on the car lighter, inhales deeply, then hands it to me. "Trust me," Danny says. "It's the *only* way."

I hit off the joint a few times. We hand it back and forth, smoking until it's gone. Danny stops the car every once in a while to nail signs to a tree or a telephone pole. I watch him through a dirty windshield, stoned.

"Let's go into town," Danny says, contemplating three signs that remain. "That's a good place. People will see it."

He turns onto a small road, barely wide enough for the Jetta.

"Where are you taking me?" I ask.

"What did I just say?" Danny asks. "Idiot."

I say, "This is the road Louis always gets lost on. I think." I'm sleepy from the pot.

"Just shut your fucking mouth for once," Danny says. "Just shut that fucking mouth for one minute, Emery."

Twenty minutes later, nothing in sight but green hills and a few farmhouses. Danny pulls over into some weeds at the side of the road. He gets out of the car now, walks over to a tree and, with the camera going, videotapes himself taking a piss. I light a cigarette, put it out. Danny's pointing the camera at the car now, waving to me. It's bright out and I'm squinting.

"What are we doing?" I ask.

Danny walks to the car, reaches in my window, takes the joint I'm holding, and lights it.

"I thought Louis said this was a shortcut," he says, looking around.

Danny gets in the driver's side, looks straight ahead with the camera.

"Where are we?" I ask.

"I don't know. Shit."

"What's that supposed to . . . mean?"

Danny takes a long pull off the joint, holds in the smoke for a while. Without exhaling, trying to hold smoke, he says, "Don't lose it."

No stations on the radio, middle of nowhere, wherever. I look at the ground move next to the car, and it seems like we're going faster than we really are. Ten minutes later we hit a main route, and Danny takes a left. Up ahead is a sign that reads WELCOME TO HISTORIC BENNINGTON, VERMONT. Danny winces, turns the car around, and heads back to Suzanna.

"I know some people who go to Bennington College," he says, looking in his rearview mirror. He shudders.

We get back to the house at almost eleven. A sign at the gate: GIANT CELEBRITY GARAGE SALE. Everyone is up; there are cars in the driveway, people on the front lawn of the house. Louis is selling everything.

"Fifty," Louis says to a tiny woman, maybe eighty years old. Her back is hunched and she is wearing a hat with flowers and a pinecone on it.

"Five dollars." She holds up five spindly fingers. "I don't know what's in the bag."

Louis says, "You don't know what's in the bag, *that's* the point. It's locked. Mystery bag. It could be gold bars in that bag."

"It could be newspaper. Or glass," the old woman says. "Ten dollars."

Louis sees me. "I'll tell you what. Here's the owner of that bag right now. Mrs. Ramsey, this is Emery Roberts."

"I'll give you five dollars for that suitcase and its contents, Mr. Roberts," the woman says, holding up five fingers again.

Danny points the camera at me. "Does 'Giant Celebrity

Garage Sale' mean the garage sale is giant, or does it mean the celebrity is giant?"

"Who's a celebrity?" the old woman asks.

Louis says, pointing to me, "This is none other than Emery Roberts."

The old woman looks me up, then down. "He's no more than six feet tall. Doesn't seem very giant to me."

"I believe the sign refers to his celebrity *status*," Louis says.

"Never heard of him," the woman says.

"That's impossible." Louis looks insulted.

"Movie actor?" the woman asks, looking at the suitcase.

"Nominated for a Golden Globe," Danny says, zooming in on the old woman. "*And* a People's Choice."

"Errol Flynn," Mrs. Ramsey says, looking me up and down again. "Now *there* was a movie actor. You I've never heard of before in my life."

Louis talks in a serious voice. "According to Pauline Kael, Emery Roberts was, quote-unquote, way too convincing as the know-nothing extraterrestrial in *Let Them Call Him Rebel*."

People are milling around the yard, going through my things. A man with muttonchops, wearing a Garfield T-shirt, holds up a Yamamoto blazer.

"Twenty dollars," Louis says to him. "Firm."

The man puts it back on the table.

"That's from the designer section, sir. That coat was worn by Emery Roberts, New Year's Eve at Eddie Murphy's place."

The man looks at me, picks the coat up again, and tries it on. The sleeves are too small for him. He fishes through his pockets and hands Louis a twenty. Louis hands the money to me.

Louis says, "You're going to need this money for lawsuits." He reaches in his back pocket and pulls out an assortment of other bills and hands them to me, crumpled up, like trash. "There's sixty-three bucks there. That's fifteen minutes with Bloom & Dekom." Louis walks over to a pile of clothes and shows a customer my shirts. The old woman is still examining my suitcase.

Jeremiah comes out the front door with some old chairs, Anne following him with a lamp and a set of skis. They set the stuff on the lawn, then go back inside for more.

"Louis . . ." I begin tentatively. "Did you save some stuff . . . for me?"

Louis gives me thumbs-up. Anne drags a steamer trunk out the front door. Danny pans the crowd with his camera. Jeremiah is handing 7-Ups to the shoppers.

"I'll give you fifteen for the suitcase," the old woman says. "And I won't go higher. No telling what's in it."

Louis starts in again. "But, madam, that's the whole point. It's a mystery grab bag suitcase. From a *celebrity* owner.

There could be important *stuff* in there. There could be *cash* in there. Celebrity cash. You're not just getting *any* suitcase here. This could be worth *thousands* someday. Maybe more. This may be the celebrity sale of the *century*. There could be valuable art in there. Picasso's."

The old woman looks at Louis, then at me. I have no idea what is in the suitcase.

"Did you ever watch 'Let's Make a Deal'?" Louis asks her. "This is door number three—"

"Young man," the woman interrupts him. "You're beginning to get on my nerves."

"Twenty," I say. "It's twenty."

She looks at me again, then smiles and opens her purse. "Ever hear of a man named Montgomery Clift?"

I nod, unsure.

"My eldest brother knew him," she says. "From his early days in the theater."

"Who's Montgomery Clift?" Danny asks.

"He was the husband on 'Bewitched,'" Louis says.

"You'll have to help me get it to the car," the old woman says, tapping the suitcase. "I'm afraid it's too heavy for a woman my age."

Louis carries the bag to her car, and the woman hands me the money.

"*You're* a celebrity?" Mrs. Ramsey squints.

"I'm afraid so," Anne says. "Pity."

"Emery's always a little bit more low-key than one expects," Danny says.

Mrs. Ramsey walks to her car, and Louis comes back.

"What was in it?" he asks.

"An old girlfriend?" I shrug. "I don't know."

"Less stuff Emery has, the happier Emery is."

A man is interested in making a deal for a Paul Smith suit and an unread copy of *Ulysses*. Research I never did involving a rock-opera version with a score by Michael Bolton.

Louis holds up four fingers.

"Will you autograph it?" the man asks me.

Louis nods. "The autograph will be two dollars extra."

High school kids walk away with a couple of chairs, the girls in the group staring at me. Louis looks at them, leering, then at me. Louis thumps his fist against his other palm.

"Nothing like a fifteen-year-old creature," Louis says.

Anne motions for me. I step around what is left of my belongings. I sign an autograph for a little girl and stop to take a picture with some guys in baseball uniforms.

"Where'd you go?" Anne asks, wiping dust off chairs.

"We ended up in Bennington," Danny says.

"You probably want to know where all this stuff came from," she says to me, then, realizing something, directs the question elsewhere.

Jeremiah comes up and pats me hard on the back. "I found it in the attic. Thought I could cash in on the *celebrity* seeker crowd. Jesus."

"Relax," Anne says. "It's okay. Right, Jeremiah?"

"Long as we don't make a habit. I mean, I could have done without the autograph stuff."

"Hey!" Nathan comes around the side of the house.

"Hey what?" Anne says. "You are so fucking annoying sometimes, Nathan. Just the sight of you annoys."

Nathan isn't wearing a shirt, and he's sweaty, hands dirty. There is a little bit of mud caked on the side of his face. "If you guys are going to fuck around, realize that in this heat I am not. Someone's got to make the situation better, and if I'm going to be the one, I would at least appreciate some respect." He looks at the ground, breathing hard, his face red.

"What's the matter, Nathan?" Anne asks. "What the hell could possibly be the matter now?"

Nathan gestures with his hand, disgusted. "Tell these people to keep their kids out of my swimming pool."

"Two points, Nathan," Jeremiah says. "One, that is not a swimming pool. Two, that is not a swimming pool."

Nathan looks at the ground and shakes his head, looks back up at all the people, milling around, sifting through the clothes and furniture and other stuff. "Keep the kids out of the hole."

*　*　*

Jeremiah pulls up old floorboards in one of the rooms downstairs. The window is open so we won't breathe dust. The air is humid and still, and as Jeremiah pulls up each piece of rotted wood floor, dust shoots up, then hangs in the air, all around us. It seems like the hottest day so far.

"Anne says you were on 'ET' last night," Jeremiah says. "Something about *This Terrible Salad.* Is that what it's actually called?"

"I think it's only playing in New York."

"When you have Monty for a father, you hear about this shit whether you want to or not," Jeremiah says.

Jeremiah struggles to get a piece of bad wood free, his face red with effort.

"It's a tiny movie," I say.

"They pay you well?"

"Scale."

Jeremiah looks at the floor, confused. "Favored nations? Why did you do it?"

"It was shooting in the south of France," I say. "Danielle wanted to go for a little vacation. Danielle loves all of the director's films. Danielle thinks he's a genius."

Jeremiah breaks wood strips over his knee. "I thought Danielle was strictly huge Hollywood movies, big salaries, points, premieres, Oliver Stone, Warner Brothers."

"Danielle wanted to go to Cannes," I say.

"Who directed it?" Jeremiah asks. "Who directed *This Terrible Salad?*"

"German guy," I say. "A German."

Jeremiah nods. "Didn't he make that movie about the mimes? For Falconer Films."

"No, that was another German," I say. A long pause. "Actually the mime movie was made by an Italian."

"You know what else Anne says was on 'Entertainment Tonight'?"

"They discovered that John Tesh is . . . Satan?"

"It was quote-unquote leaked to the press that you left," Jeremiah says. "Something like that. Hurley was on 'Arsenio' plugging some kind of Save the Soft-Shell Crab Benefit and"—Jeremiah pauses—"ducking questions about you."

Gladys comes in with a plate of sun-dried tomato and arugula sandwiches and bottles of Evian. She sets them down and looks at the dust, the mess, into the little hole. She walks out, shaking her head, laughing, "My goodness."

"You're money," Jeremiah says. "You *are* money, Emery. People care about where the money is."

"I am . . . money," I say.

"My father called," Jeremiah says. "Last night. Also Danielle and Hurley's agent."

"Uh-huh," I say.

"Expected. I'm actually surprised it wasn't sooner." Jeremiah tugs at another board.

"And . . . were they nice?"

He shakes his head, gulps water from a bottle. "I told them I hadn't seen you."

"They know," I say, standing up to stretch.

Jeremiah shrugs. "Probably."

Nathan comes into the room with two shovels and hands Jeremiah one. "I thought you were helping today."

"No," Jeremiah says, eating a sandwich.

"No one helps and this thing'll take forever," Nathan says, pissed off. "Goddammit, it's a hundred and fifty degrees out."

"Take a cold shower," Jeremiah says.

"I'm improving your property," Nathan says.

"I suppose you have a point," Jeremiah says, sucking his hand, a splinter. "I'm just not getting it."

Louis and Danny and I are in town at Dunkin' Donuts. Danny has the camera sitting on the table, trying to videotape locals without their noticing. Louis rummages through a bag of tapes and magazines just bought at the Record Rack.

"My boy Petty's an elder statesman," Louis says.

"Tom Petty?" I ask.

Louis lights a cigarette, nods. "Into the great wide open—rebel without a clue."

Danny gets up and starts taping a kid playing a video game. The kid looks over his shoulder every once in a while, uncomfortable, loses men because of it.

"And these guys," Louis says, holding up Guns N' Roses. "Ugly. But do they get creatures or what? Look at the caliber of creature in their videos. My boy Axl's got it down. Even Slash. Slash has it down."

"Axl," I say, lighting a cigarette. "Axl Rose? Slash?"

"Yes, Axl Rose." Louis coughs, rolls his eyes. "These are people *you* know, Emery. *You* party with Slash. *You* share creatures with Axl."

Louis pulls magazines from the bag, goes through them, giggling at *GQ*.

"Don't do this," I say.

Louis holds it up, my face on the cover, smirking, hair slicked back, ridiculous.

"Don't," I say.

Louis flips through it. "Where's the fashion spread? Where's the posing?" He finds the article. "Aha."

Louis reads, giggling. Danny has the camera pointed at the girl behind the counter. "What's the profit margin on the glazed?" he's asking. The girl looks embarrassed, smiles at me, blushes. I rub my eyes, mildly grossed out.

Louis says, "Here's a nice one."

He shows me a picture of myself, wearing an Armani tux, standing hip-deep in the ocean. I am holding a dead fish, pretending it's alive. Some of the shots were taken with Ray-Bans; some weren't. This is a picture without Ray-Bans. Herb Ritts.

"Please," I say. "I said please."

"Emery," Danny calls over from the counter, camera now pointed at me. "This is Brandy, right?" Danny looks at her, and Brandy nods, not taking her eyes off me.

I sort of wave, nod, grimace, whatever.

"Brandy wants to know if we're up here filming anything."

"Yeah—the Abe Vigoda story," Louis mutters, studying the magazine.

"Abe Vigoda. Dead or alive," Danny says. "You make the call."

"If Emery's playing him," Louis says, "dead."

Danny turns the camera back on Brandy and starts questioning her about doughnuts again.

"Danny's got a good creature scam going with that camera," Louis says. "Like that guy in New York, asks women to take off their clothes for him."

Some locals walk by the window and recognize me. They run ahead and get their friends and come back to look at me. The guy from the D who asked if I was from around here waves his friends off, walks ahead, down the street. The others stay and watch.

"Becky's coming up with her kid tomorrow," Louis says, then adds, casually, "because they closed down production."

"Why?"

"To see her man," Louis says. "For lovin' good fun with me." He thumps his fist against his other palm.

"You don't think she's already been getting that?" I say. "With Hurley Thompson and Briston Jr. running around the set? And Monty?"

"If you're trying to get a rise here, piss me off or something, it won't work," Louis says. "I've got you. In *GQ.*"

I shrug.

"You think Monty would dog her?"

"Yes," I say.

"What about Briston Jr.?" Louis asks.

"Yes," I say. "I think Briston Jr. has fucked your girl-friend, Becky."

The crowd grows.

"Let's leave," Danny says.

"Remind me to ask Jeremiah," Louis says.

"Jeremiah doesn't like talking about the business," I say.

"Or as the people in the business call it, the industry," Louis says. "Jesus, you look stupid in these pictures."

ACT II

Nathan stands in the hole, digging. Danny videotapes him, asking questions Nathan doesn't answer.

"Get him away from me," Nathan says. "Emery, *do* something."

"He won't go," I say to Nathan.

"Wild horses couldn't drag me away from Emery," Danny says. "Cindy Crawford couldn't drag me away from Emery."

"What if I got you a gig as a segment director on 'Runaway with the Rich and Famous'?" Nathan asks. "You could work with people like Donna Mills and Lorenzo Lamas. Champagne wishes and caviar dreams?"

"Nope." Danny plays with the focus. "I have to live my life by a certain minimum moral standard."

Nathan continues to shovel dirt. "What about a job as assistant to Rowdy Herrington on *Road House 2?*"

"Now you're talking," Danny says.

I sigh, watch Nathan push the shovel into the ground with his foot.

Louis comes around the back, hair slicked, shaven. Danny whistles and Louis flips Danny off with both hands.

"Becky's coming up today?" Danny says. "With the kid?"

Louis looks at his watch. "Any minute."

"New character," Danny says. "New subject."

"Creature," Louis says.

Louis sits and waits, watching Nathan dig for a while. Danny circles the hole, videotaping us. Half an hour later Becky's taxi pulls up the driveway, and Louis gets up, stubs out a joint, tries to calm down.

Becky gets out of the car and hugs Louis. Louis opens the passenger door and undoes Enzo from the portable baby seat, then holds him in the air, studying the child. Gladys comes out and takes the baby inside.

Nathan climbs out of the hole and starts to fill a wheelbarrow. The sky gets dark as clouds block the sun. My shadow, which I've been studying, disappears, blends in with the dirt. Louis and Becky walk over, and Becky offers an air kiss. Becky and I slept together during the shooting of *Sun City*, the majority of the time in a motel room at the edge of Death Valley. "Not exactly an inappropriate place to have sex with you," Becky said the seventh day of shooting.

"Everyone's looking for Emery," Becky says, squeezing my hand. "What happened?"

Louis puts his arms around her from behind, protectively. "He's just here now, that's all."

"But . . ." Becky starts, looking pissed off, confused.

"Monty shut down production. Hurley feels dissed. Everyone's nuts."

"He quit," Louis says.

"But what about . . ." Becky doesn't finish, exhales. "They need you for those last four scenes."

"Tell them to use a body double," Danny says, taping.

"Don't you think it's kind of fucked?" Becky asks. "Other people have jobs and you're not letting it happen?"

"He has his reasons," Louis says, pointing a finger at Becky. "And damn good reasons, too."

"No smoking in the house," Danny says. "Jeremiah's rule number one."

"You're the star," Becky says to me. "You are the star."

Louis makes a face, sticks out his tongue. In a few seconds it's raining and Anne runs out of the house, her palms turned upward.

"This ought to cool you off," Danny calls to Nathan, camera pointed at Anne.

"Summer storms are over in minutes," Nathan says, snapping his fingers. "Like that."

"What are you two doing?" Becky asks, moving toward the house, glancing at the hole. "Hi, Nathan."

The rain comes down softer. Becky's affair with Nathan started sometime near the end of ours. It lasted just as long.

"We're digging a swimming pool," Nathan says, not looking up.

"Didn't know you were that shallow," Becky jokes.

Louis tries to smile.

"Let's get out of this rain," he says to her.

Louis is driving home from the D. Becky is in the passenger seat, talking about Oahu, the north shore where she used to live with her ex-husband, a surf film director named Sinjin. Louis doesn't seem to want to hear this, fiddles with the radio. Anne is in the backseat with me.

"Don't worry about locals, Emery," Becky says. "Locals anywhere are generally nice people. Especially to people like you. It's just that it's their place. It's where they live and they don't want strangers fucking anything up." Becky pauses. "To put it in a way you would all understand, it's kind of like Morton's."

Everyone takes this in, or maybe no one is listening.

"On the north shore no one gave me and Sinj any trouble," Becky says.

"I think the locals in Hawaii are a lot different from the ones here. Over there I heard they're very territorial. It's not such a safe place for hoolies." Louis says this.

Becky lights a cigarette.

"What's a hoolie?" Anne asks, staring out the window, drunk.

"Howlie," Becky says. "It means a mainlander."

"It means a white person," Louis says.

"No one's bothered you, have they, Emery?" Anne asks.

"He's scared of the potential for trouble," Louis says. "Emery's scared for his face. An actor's got to protect his face."

"I've met some of the locals," Anne says. "But no money. You won't like them."

"Louis doesn't have money," Becky says, staring out the windshield.

"Exactly," Anne says quietly.

"What do you mean?" Louis says. "I have money. I don't have Emery money, but I have money."

"I don't want to talk about locals or Sinjin or Morton's or any of this," Anne moans. "Okay?"

"I just don't want Emery uptight when nothing's going to happen," Becky says, rolling down a window.

Anne takes a swig from a bottle. As Louis rounds a turn very fast, some scotch spills down the side of her cheek.

"Louis," Anne says. "Goddammit, slow down."

"Give me the bottle," Louis says. Anne reluctantly hands it to Louis. He finishes the last inch.

"Are we almost home?" Becky asks. "Please don't say I don't know."

"I don't know," Louis says, his voice raspy from the liquor.

"We're lost?" Anne says, taking hold of my hand. "Oh God, not again. Don't tell me we're lost again."

"What do you think?" Louis says. "Jesus, Anne. You need help."

Louis pulls over to the side of the road and kills the engine, turns off the lights. It is pitch-black out.

"We've got the car, middle of nowhere, stars in the sky. Creatures on a dark and lovely night."

"Do *not* call me a creature," Becky says. "I've warned you about that."

"It's a night made for love," Louis says. "Love of a particularly creaturish nature."

"I say we get out of the car," Anne says. "Immediately."

"Go ahead." Louis smiles evilly. "You're not going to find the local chapter of NOW anywhere around here to save you."

We walk out into a field. Louis brings his flask, drinking from it while he leads. He trips a couple of times in the dark, but we manage to get maybe fifty yards from the road. Louis sits down on the grass. Becky and Anne remain standing. We look up at the sky and stare for a while, no one saying a word. In the distance there are flashes of lightning.

Louis gets up and I follow him to a tree. Complete darkness.

Anne and Becky smoke cigarettes, and the embers glow

in the dark, move around. The clouds get closer, the lightning more frequent; a wind starts to blow.

"People called again for you today," Louis says, pissing. "Monty, Danielle, others."

"Becky told them?" I ask.

"I think they probably just figured it out."

I picture the remains of my world in midair, myself apart from it. Progress, money, reality.

"Was it easy to figure out, Louis?" I ask.

"A friend of Nathan's out there told him it was in the trades," Louis says. "A friend."

The sound of thunder echoes and lightning hits on the other side of the hill.

"Something like 'City prod shut down. Where is Roberts? Warner's stox down' or something. Tradespeak."

Raindrops start to fall, and Becky's and Anne's cigarettes move back to the car. One slips. I hear a yelp.

"Come on, you guys," Becky calls.

"They want to go?" Louis mutters. "Let them walk."

I see the girls when another bolt of lightning hits. They are almost to the car.

After thunder I hear one of them yell, "Let's *go*, boys."

The rain starts to fall harder. Louis and I are soaked.

"Fuck 'em," Louis says. "Let them wait."

* * *

I take a shower and then I'm downstairs in front of the TV. Jeremiah is watching the news. Louis paints Becky's toenails, while Becky stares at the baby.

"You just missed yourself," Louis says. "Another Emery story."

Jeremiah says, "This is getting out of hand."

"You should go back," Becky says, making a face at the baby.

"A reporter called today," Jeremiah says, irritated. "From the *Suzanna Star*. Wants to write an article about what you're doing up here. This is getting out of hand."

"Tell them he's not here," Louis says. "Shit, Jeremiah."

"The reporter saw him," Jeremiah says. "At your little garage sale. The reporter bought an autographed bottle of Ramblosa."

Anne comes in with Danny and bags of Chinese food.

Danny unpacks the food, opens boxes, and eats with his fingers. "We had to go all the way to town for this stuff. No one delivers in this burg. This is *not* civilization."

"They want to do a story on Emery," Becky says to Anne. "The *Suzanna Star*."

"Fuck that," Jeremiah says. "That's all I need is some reporter sticking his nose up Emery's ass, wanting pictures and quotes."

"Emery likes people sticking their noses up his ass," Danny says.

"He's *not* here," Louis says, emphatic.

"How can you say that?" Becky blows on Enzo's face. No one answers her.

"Hold still," Louis says. "Put Enzo down."

Becky lets Enzo crawl on the floor. He crawls to the TV, sits in front of it, stares.

"No celebrity interviews. None," Jeremiah says.

Becky asks, "What if they want to talk to me?"

Louis asks, "Why would they want to talk to you when they could have Emery?"

"That's not very nice," Anne says, smiling.

"Fuck nice," Danny says. "This is Hollywood."

"This is *not* Hollywood!" Jeremiah says. "This is something entirely different. I don't know what it is, but it's not Hollywood. Fuck that. This is this, Emery. This isn't something else here. This is this."

Jeremiah tosses the remote to Anne and storms out of the room. Anne calmly changes the channel.

"This is this?" Louis says, blinking. "What the hell is that supposed to mean? This is this. An Emeryism."

"Where's Nathan?" Becky asks. "Where's poolboy?"

"Where do you think?" Danny says. "Turtle hunting. A night hunt."

"What's Jeremiah's problem?" Louis asks. "This is this?"

"Doesn't want to 'ruin' it up here," Anne says, giggling.

"Ruin what?" Becky says. "There's nothing to ruin. I mean, no offense."

Anne takes my hand before announcing: "Monty called. He's in New York. Monty is coming up in a few days. Maybe sooner."

"He knows I'm here?" I ask.

Enzo talks to the TV. "Gapjsh!"

At the lake Louis tries to get a fire going in the hibachi, but it isn't working. Nathan stands in the boat, BB gun pointed at the water. Danny videotapes Nathan. Anne and Becky and I are on our backs in the sun, tanning, and Enzo is in his crib, asleep.

"Got to practice," Louis says.

"For what?" Becky asks.

"Fourth of July," Louis says. "Need to hone my skills as a barbecueist."

"The fire's the most important element," Becky says.

Anne sits up and rubs sunblock on my chest, without me asking her to.

"You shouldn't leave," Anne says.

"Yeah," Louis says. "Stay. You're a barrel of laughs, Emery."

"I promise Monty won't bother you." Anne continues to rub lotion on my chest.

"He'll be mad," Louis says. "Jeremiah'll be mad. Everyone will be mad at him. But big fucking deal. It's a mad mad mad mad mad mad world."

"I won't be mad," Anne says. "Emery's making it . . . fun here. Otherwise what is there? Mosquitoes. Ants. Jeremiah hammering at things all day long. Louis's shitty driving. Danny and his soon-to-be-torched camcorder?"

A shot rings out over the lake. Danny laughs.

I get up because Anne's rubbing is making me uncomfortable in this heat. Louis gives up on the hibachi and throws a Frisbee, which I catch and hand to Anne. They play catch for a while. Becky puts sunblock on the sleeping baby.

"Watch this," Louis says. He tries to throw the Frisbee from under his leg. The Frisbee ends up in the water, a few feet from shore.

"Don't do it," Nathan yells, waving his arms. "Don't go in."

"It's only right here." Louis points. "I don't think it's a problem."

"You're a fool," Nathan calls from the boat. "You'll see."

Louis kicks off his tennis shoes and steps into the green water. He picks up the Frisbee and throws it back to Anne, who holds the Frisbee, staring at it blankly.

"See?" Louis says to Nathan. "No sharks in the shallow end."

"Inspect the Frisbee for bite marks," Nathan yells.

Nathan turns his attention to the water next to the boat and lets off a couple of rounds, then a couple more. Danny still has the camera pointed at me.

"Let's wake up the baby," Louis says. "The little guy sleeps too much."

"Don't," Becky warns.

"Enzo," Louis says softly. "Enzo. Time to get up. Louis is going to teach you about the real world."

"Stop it," Becky whispers. "What does a failed agent know about the real world anyway?"

"Uncalled for, Becky." Anne giggles.

"We could offer Enzo to the turtles," Louis says, picking up the baby, who smiles, sleepily. "As a sacrifice or a tribute. Maybe then we could all swim."

Louis holds Enzo horizontally and runs with him toward the water. At the last minute, at the edge of the waterline, Louis swings the baby up in the air. Enzo laughs.

"Louis," Becky warns.

"Relax," Louis says, looking at the kid. "We're not going to feed Enzo baby to the turtles, are we? Oh yes we are."

Louis runs with the baby again toward the water and lifts him high at the last minute. Anne comes over to me with my shoes.

"I want to show you something," she says.

I put on my sneakers and we walk an uphill path. Anne

hums music that is sort of familiar-sounding. The path ends and we make our way through trees, bushes, tall grass. A horsefly buzzes around my head and lands. We come to a clearing; a huge boulder, we sit in the shade beside it.

Anne pushes on my shoulders so that I'm lying down and rubs my chest again, kissing, sucking my nipples. Her hand moves down to my swim trunks, underneath, stroking, and after a while I'm stiff. I feel her mouth on mine, then a breast. Anne takes off my trunks and then her clothes. I'm on my back, and she gets on top of me and starts to move.

Later, I wake up. Anne puts on her bikini bottom. I shield my eyes from the sun, still very bright. I'm out in the middle of the open, no clothes on, just sneakers. Mosquito bites run up and down my arms. I turn my back to Anne as I pull on my trunks. But she puts her arms around my neck, her bare chest up against mine. Anne kisses my shoulder and lays her head there, and I stand that way for a few minutes. When she lets go, I lace my shoes. Anne climbs up on the rock and puts on her T-shirt. She points. "You can see the lake from here." I finish tying my shoes and begin climbing the rock to where she stands. When I get to the top of the rock and stand next to her, there is only room for one, really, and we have to hold on to each other for balance.

"What's mama doin'? What's mama doin'?" Louis is imitating a woman's high voice. He clears his throat and spits. He puts a shovelful of dirt into a wheelbarrow that I'm standing next to.

"She doesn't say that," Nathan says. "Becky does *not* say that."

Louis wipes the sweat off his forehead with a red bandanna. "How would you know?"

"Does she?" Nathan asks innocently.

Louis holds up a hand. "Swear to God if there is one."

"What's mama doing?" Nathan asks, appalled. "No way."

"What's mama doin'? What's mama doin'?" Louis says in a high voice again. "She gets on top of me and she holds the kid in front of her and smiles at him. What's mama doin'? And then she puts him down again, starts grinding hard. Fast." Louis slaps his palm.

"Sounds serious, Louis," Nathan says. "I don't want to know."

"I couldn't come," Louis says. "About lost my hard-on."

Nathan shakes his head.

"And she cries," Louis says, confused. "She gets off, then cries right afterward. Scared the bejesus out of me."

"Maybe she cries because you like to beat the shit out of her," I say nervously.

Louis glares, then tries to ignore this comment.

We walk with the wheelbarrow, over to a pile of dirt near what Nathan now calls the "deep end." Louis empties it and then shovels more dirt, higher onto the pile, aggressively, silent.

"We'll be cool soon enough," Nathan says from the hole. "Believe me, heat's gonna seem like nothing."

"Yeah," Louis says. "And that spec script you wrote about the haunted outhouse is going to go for two million."

"His agent's asking one-point-five," someone says.

Nathan's head disappears behind the edge of the hole. Dirt comes flying off his shovel over the side. Nathan's head comes up again, and he looks at us, breathing hard. He wipes his forehead with his hand, leaving a brown stripe. I think about telling Louis something else, but don't.

"Why am I the only one helping?" Louis asks, then at me: "What about that, asshole?"

"The kid was here," Nathan says accusingly. "With Becky this morning. He had his little plastic shovel."

Louis seems in a daze, stares out in the distance at nothing.

Nathan says, "I've been giving it thought. I think you guys would be more inclined to help out. I mean, your heart would be more into it if you had some sort of incentive."

"What are you offering? MCA stock?" Louis mutters.

I laugh hard at this.

"No, an incentive," Nathan says. "Reality. Viability."

"Can't wait for Nathan's announcement," Louis says, monotone. "Cash reward?"

I swat at a mosquito—a smear of blood.

Nathan says, leaning on his shovel, "I am the foreman of the project."

"Correction," Louis says. "The only one who cares."

"Let me finish," Nathan says. "I'm the foreman of this building site, and I thought you would become more involved if you had some measure of responsibility."

Louis looks annoyed. "Digging site. *Digging.* You said *building* site, but that's wrong. Building refers to growth upward. Digging is what we're doing. Not building."

The heat is almost unbearable, the air is so thick. Nathan is getting frustrated.

"Whatever. What I was saying was that maybe you two would enjoy a little something extra, a little something that says I'm involved here. That says, 'This is my pool, too.' "

"And what's that?" Louis asks. "An inflatable raft? Goggles?"

A big brown car cruises up the driveway. It stops and Jeremiah meets it. A huge man steps out, a linebacker, someone who makes Jeremiah look like Jeffrey Katzenberg. He says something to Jeremiah and holds out his hand to shake. Jeremiah doesn't shake the hand. The big man smiles, looks over at me, squints.

"I was thinking that I should appoint you assistant foreman." Nathan smiles.

"I don't like the sound of 'assistant,' " Louis says.

I am looking at Jeremiah argue with the big man, who is calm, nodding his head.

Louis says, "You need to come up with something better."

Jeremiah starts heading this way, looking at me the whole time.

"How about deputy foreman?" Nathan asks.

"How about executive producer?" Louis asks back.

Jeremiah grabs my arm. "See that ape over there?"

"Over there?"

"My father sent him up. Says you need a bodyguard."

"I thought your last name was Factor," Louis says. "Not Gotti."

Jeremiah says, "This guy, Mikey, has been instructed to watch you, keep you safe until my father gets here."

"Monty's holding Emery prisoner?" Louis asks.

"You want to go kick his ass or something?" Jeremiah says.

"Jeremiah, you're such a big boring loudmouth," Louis mutters. "No, I don't want to kick his ass."

"I told you," Jeremiah says. "What's the first thing I told you? I want no Hollywood bullshit up here."

"This is this," Louis says, smirking. "Remember that?"

"And what happens?" Jeremiah says. *"This* happens."

"What? He's not going to let Emery leave?" Louis asks derisively. "Right."

"Looks that way," Jeremiah says, jaw set tight. "It fucking looks that way."

"Deputy Foreman Louis," Louis says. "Says it's quitting time at the plant. Beer break."

"So he works for you?" Nathan asks Jeremiah.

"He works for Monty."

"But kind of indirectly he does, right? Like for the family?" Nathan looks over at the big man.

"What, Nathan?" Jeremiah says. "What is your fucking point?"

"Do you think we could put him to work?" Nathan asks. "Digging?"

Jeremiah says, "I don't know what the hell is happening."

A raindrop hits my arm.

"Quitting time, beer time," Louis says, looking up.

"What do you mean, quitting time?" Nathan asks.

"Emery might have his legs broken by this ape over there. I want to get a good seat. Definitely quitting time."

Louis and I walk into the house, and I hear Nathan and Jeremiah start bickering over something. In the kitchen Louis opens beer. For a minute: silence.

"If I were you, I'd seriously cut the shitty remarks about my so-called treatment of that whore upstairs," Louis says.

"What are you going to do about it?" I ask, after a pause.

"Louis moves closer," Louis says, moving closer. "I'll

break your fucking legs before the goon gets his chance."
Louis sips his beer.

Out of the corner of my eye I see the big man, Mikey,
in the hall, on the phone, watching us.

"Don't doubt it," Louis says, raising the beer to Mikey.

It has been raining since dawn, but the pool is worked on
anyway. Mikey, too. Nathan thinks it's "fun" to order Mikey
around. As it gets dark, the rain stops. It is still hot, humid,
and bugs are out in swarms.

We drive down to the D to cool off, drinking watery
Rolling Rock. Mikey stands in the corner, sipping bottled
water, and Danny has the camera pointed at him. Mikey ignores it and keeps his eyes fixed on me.

Becky left Enzo with Gladys, and she and Louis are
playing pool. Jeremiah and Nathan sit at a booth and watch
Mikey. Anne chooses a slow song on the jukebox, the Eagles,
and pulls me out onto the dance floor. I don't want to dance
with Anne, so I just lean against her and we sort of move
around, sweating.

Danny goes over to the Triv Whiz video game and tapes
the screen as he plays.

The door to the D opens and locals walk in. They act like
they've been drinking. One of them tips over a chair, pretends
it's an accident. Mikey goes into the bathroom.

"Now's your chance," Anne says. "Watchdog's gone."

"I don't know."

"My father is crazy." Anne sighs. "Not cool at all."

"Monty's pretty serious about business," I say.

"Richie." The bartender warns the guy who tipped the chair. He walks over to set it right.

Anne looks up to see Louis down his Sea Breeze. Mikey comes back and stands in the corner, looking at me.

"Jesus, he's big," Anne says admiringly. "Dad's very thorough."

The locals sit at a table, except for one, who stands next to the bar, staring at me. He sort of sways. I look to Mikey, who is watching Danny. The townie guy moves closer to Anne, downs a shot of something.

"You," he says to me. "I know who you are now."

He doesn't shake my hand, sort of laughs.

"I saw you fight," he says. "In that FBI movie."

I nod.

"You're a pretty good hitter, huh?"

"It's all staged," I say, looking for Mikey.

"No," the townie says. "I saw you hit a guy right in the jaw. For real."

"Stunt men," I say.

In one swift, surprisingly graceful movement, he grabs Anne's arm and swings her around so that she faces him and starts dancing with her. Anne tries to break free.

The other townies get up, some of them laughing.

The townie looks at me. "May I?" he asks, smiling.

"I don't think so," I say, finally, unable to move.

Anne looks pissed and pulls away from the townie and glares at me.

The townie holds out his hand. "No hard feelings? Mr. Emery Roberts."

I shake his hand. The grip is tight.

"Oh, great," Anne says. "Shake his hand, Emery."

The townie walks back to his table. Women walk in, locals. They sit with the men. The townie kisses one of them, looks at me. I sit with Jeremiah.

"Problems?" Jeremiah asks.

"Don't worry," Nathan says. "We're drunk, too. Besides, we've got Mikey there. I like Mikey. In fact, Mikey is the only one here I like."

"So go fuck him," Jeremiah says, staring into his drink.

"Who said I fuck people I like?" Nathan asks. "Who started that rumor?"

"Thanks for getting me out of that," Anne says to me.

Louis comes over with more drinks and hands me one. I down it fast and take another from the tray. The townie waves, wants me to come over. He has his arm around a girl and says something to her. Laughing, the townie waves me over again.

"Come on, Mr. Movie Star," he shouts. "Nothing's gonna happen to you."

"Don't let them hit your face," Nathan says. "Your face is your fortune."

With the help of four Sea Breezes I walk over to the locals, looking over my shoulder at Mikey, who is watching me. When I get to their table, everyone is silent, smiling.

"I'm Tom," the townie says. "I want you to meet my girlfriend, Lizzie."

Lizzie stares at me, smiles. "Nice to meet you."

"She knows who you are, pretty boy," Tom says.

They all laugh.

"Why don't you join us for a drink?" Lizzie asks.

Tom says, "You must be pretty loaded. Buy us a drink."

"I can't," I say, looking at Mikey. "We're about to . . . take off anyway."

"Sure?" Tom says.

Tom looks at Lizzie, who looks at me.

"Positive," I say. "Maybe some other time."

I start to walk away, but Tom gets up and taps my shoulder.

"I want you to kiss my girlfriend," he says.

I stand there.

"She's always going off on how good-looking your mouth is," he says, beer-fueled. "I want you to kiss her. As a present."

I can't say anything.

"What?" Tom says. "She's not good enough for you? She's too ugly for a pretty mouth like you?"

"That's not it," I say, walking away. "I just don't . . . kiss people."

"You saying she's not pretty enough?"

"Tom," Lizzie says, embarrassed.

"Shut up," he says to her. "You always wanted to kiss him, I'm going to get him to kiss you."

I wave to get Mikey's attention. Mikey comes walking over. I feel a pull on my shoulder, turning me around. Tom swings but misses. His other fist, however, comes at me from the other direction, strikes me in the neck. Two other townies are up now along with Nathan and Jeremiah and Louis. Anne and Becky are screaming, and Tom elbows me in the ribs, tries to force me into a headlock. Mikey pushes Tom away from me.

The bartender kicks the locals out. Jeremiah and Louis play pool. Nathan leaves to take Becky back. Danny plays Triv Whiz, and Mikey stands by the door, not a hair out of place, guarding it.

"Big man came in handy," Louis says. "My boy Mikey."

"All of you boys okay?" Anne asks.

Her hand goes over a bruise and I wince.

"Stop," I say, irritated. "Jesus."

"Fine," she says. Anne goes to a booth and sits down alone.

Jeremiah says, patting my shoulder, "Nice, Emery. Really glad you could make it up here."

As he walks away, I say, "I didn't start this."

It is very early in the morning. I wake up outdoors, in an alley next to the D. Mikey sits up against the side of the building, rubbing his eyes.

"Where am I?" I ask.

A dog walks by me, sniffs, growls a little. My fly is open. There is a scrape on my arm, dried blood. My head aches and I'm nauseous. I can feel the places on my body where I was hit last night: my neck, my ribs, the side of my face, all swollen.

"You were drinking," Mikey says. "You came here and passed out."

"They left me?" I ask.

"I stayed." Mikey yawns. "I'm here."

I try to stand up, straighten my shirt, which reeks like beer and maybe a little like vomit, though I see none around me. Mikey and I walk around the corner. The D is closed, but Mikey checks the door anyway.

"That way." Mikey points to a brown car down the street.

We walk slowly toward it. I find it hard to keep my balance since I feel so bad.

"Why didn't you take me home?" I ask.

"I was told not to interfere," Mikey says. "Just keep an eye."

"What if I paid you," I say. "What if I gave you what Monty's giving you?"

Mikey shakes his head, doesn't smile.

When we are almost to the car, a Suzanna policeman drives by, looking us over. The patrol car makes a U-turn and comes back our way, following us slowly. The cop pulls over and gets out.

"Good morning," Mikey says.

"Can I see some ID?"

Mikey pulls out his wallet and hands it to the cop. I feel my pockets, nothing.

The cop says to me, "I know who you are."

He hands Mikey back his wallet.

"I hear there was a little trouble here last night," the cop says. "Everything get squared up?"

Mikey says, "I don't think there'll be any more problems."

"When you're guests in someone else's town," the cop says slowly, "you have to be a little careful about what you say and do. You don't want to ruffle anyone's feathers."

I scratch some dried vomit off my collar.

"I understand someone of your stature and notoriety, Mr. Roberts, getting the occasional challenge."

"It happens all the time," Mikey says.

I light a cigarette and take a drag that almost makes me sick again. I toss it at my feet, stamping it out. The cop lowers his sunglasses and looks at me, then smiles, sort of. He raises his sunglasses, then, after a while, gets in his car.

"Happy Fourth," the cop says. "Have a safe one." The police car drives off slowly.

We get in Mikey's car, I sit in the back, and Mikey hits autolock. Mikey drives to Jeremiah's.

Mikey comes around and opens the door for me. I step out of the car, still dizzy, and head toward the front of the house. Danny stands on the porch, pointing the camera at my face.

"Emery has had a long night," Mikey says.

Louis is in the kitchen, mixing a pink drink. He raises it, offering it to me.

"Is there vodka in that? Emery wonders," Louis says. "Emery stares at the glass, a pained look on his face, and nods."

"Get it away from me." I can barely speak.

"Hair of the dog," Louis says after sipping.

"You were shit-faced and kept insulting people," Danny says.

"I don't remember."

"You 'broke up' with Anne."

"I'm going to get some sleep," Mikey says. "If you want to know where I am."

"I'm going to run away the minute you're gone," I say.

"Oh, right," Mikey says, climbing the stairs.

Upstairs I stand in front of Anne's room for a long time before knocking. Anne comes up the hall, from the shower, hair wet, wearing only a towel.

"Monty's due around four," she says. "I think Danielle's with him."

I watch her open the door.

"You stink," Anne says, once in her room, sniffing me. "If they see you like this, they're going to think you're on a bender again. And we don't want a replay of that part of Emery's life, do we?"

"Don't worry. Not in the mood," I say, looking at myself in the mirror.

"That pretty much sums up your attitude concerning all things," Anne says.

"Louis said that I 'broke up' with you last night," I say, watching Anne pull a blouse on.

"Broke up from what?" Anne laughs.

"From . . . each other?" I say, unsure.

"Emery, we've known each other how long?" Anne asks, sighing. "How long has it been, Emery?"

"I don't know," I say.

"Since tenth grade," she says. "We've known each other since we were sixteen."

I shrug.

"I know about Danielle," Anne says. "I'm just not understanding why."

I start to say something but don't.

"I mean, I know why," Anne says. "I don't know. What did I expect?" Anne looks at her face in the mirror, purses her lips for a second. "And everyone knows about Becky. Louis knows about Becky."

"Louis enjoys . . . beating Becky up," I say, swallowing. "He likes it, Anne."

"I'd like to beat Becky up, too," Anne says, combing out her hair. "In fact, I'd like to rip her eyeballs out."

It's so humid in Anne's room right now that I can barely move. I take a Xanax, dry.

"Girlfriend?" Anne finally forces a laugh. "Why would anyone want to be your girlfriend?"

It is afternoon when I wake up. While I'm drinking water and taking Valium, a wave of dizziness comes over me but passes. Out the window of my room I see everyone getting settled in the backyard. Louis sets up a picnic table and a barbecue. The water cooler is out there, the bottle filled with pink liquid, Sea Breeze.

I stay in the shower for a long time. I make it go cold before turning off the water. I dry myself off, shivering, get dressed.

In the wall room, people have painted new graffiti. There is a mosquito on the wall, stuck in paint. Someone has drawn a circle around it and written

deadbug

I wander around the house, down past the TV room, out the back door. Everyone stops talking. Monty and Danielle are standing there.

"There he is," Monty says. "How's my little fugitive?"

I try to smile. Danielle kisses me, takes my hand. Everyone starts talking again; the party goes on. Danny has the camera going, and he's circling us.

"You had us worried," Danielle says. "But we found you."

"Hope Mikey didn't get in your way," Monty says, squeezing my shoulder.

Jeremiah comes up and stands next to his father.

"Jeremiah," Monty says. "The house coming along? The remodel?"

"Fine," he says.

Monty points to the pool site. "Putting in a new septic tank?"

"Digging it with our own bare hands," Jeremiah says.

"Charming," Danielle says.

Monty whispers to me. "Isn't that your assistant?"

I nod. I'm wearing sunglasses.

"Tell him to get that fucking camera out of my face, will you?"

"The Sea Breeze is ready," Louis announces, filling a plastic cup from the water dispenser.

Jeremiah looks at the ground, and Anne walks over with a tray of crackers, cheese, and a drink for me. "From Louis," she says.

Monty looks over the cheese. "This real Vermont?" and then to me: "And I hope that's a nonalcoholic beverage, my little friend."

Anne shrugs. "Bought it at the Price Chopper."

"Juice," I say, coughing.

"Louis says he makes them strong because America is strong." Anne sighs. "But that for Emery he only used, uh, nonalcoholic Stoli."

"When's your vacation over?" Monty asks me. "When can we get back to business?"

"He's helping fix up the house," Jeremiah says.

"Emery's actually helping someone *do* something?" Monty asks dubiously. "And it's *what?* Fixing a house?"

"The production's been shut down," Danielle says.

"Becky told us," Anne says.

POOL

"Becky," Monty says. "Wonderful girl."

"How long are you here for, Monty?" Jeremiah asks.

"You want to get rid of me so soon?" Monty says, smiling. "My son hasn't seen me in six months and he's already sick of me in five minutes."

Danielle says, "Oh, they're glad you're here."

"I just want to see my kids," Monty says. "What's wrong with wanting to see my fucking kids?"

"Let's not talk about this right this minute," Danielle says.

"Let's not," Jeremiah says. "Ever."

Monty sips his drink.

Monty and Danielle walk around the pool hole, conferring quietly with each other, every once in a while looking over at me. The rest of us sit at a picnic table and watch Louis barbecue. When the food is done cooking, everyone sits down to eat. Monty and Danielle get ready to leave soon after.

"We're in town", Monty says, stepping into a limousine. "At an inn called—at some inn called . . . oh, shit, what's it called?"

"It's called The Inn," Danielle says.

"Right," Monty says. "We're staying at an inn called The Inn."

"We'll come by tomorrow, Emery." Danielle squeezes my hand, kissing me on the mouth.

I'm watching Louis bite into a hot dog.

After Monty and Danielle leave, someone passes around a joint.

"I don't want them up here," Jeremiah says after a while.

"You think I do?" Anne says.

"How did they find Emery?" Danny asks. "Anyone?"

"They have their ways," Louis says. "Emery couldn't hide from this world if he jumped into a volcano."

Nathan nods. "Do you think Monty and Danielle would be interested in helping with the pool?"

No one answers him. Danny points the camera at me.

"First you, now them," Jeremiah says tiredly. "Pretty soon we'll have a Spago in Suzanna. A *Variety* bureau office. A fucking Versace boutique."

"They'll find you," Louis says, hitting off a joint. "They always catch up."

"You can't leave," Jeremiah says, stoned, staring off in the distance. "Now it's too late."

"It was too late a week ago," Anne says.

In Louis's car, driving around in the middle of nowhere, trying to find our way home in the dark, Louis is drunk and still talking about Monty and Danielle and Mikey, how much they make everyone tense. Louis turns around a lot while he drives, directing the comments to Anne in the backseat, his eyes not on the road.

"Wait a minute," Louis says. "That sign up there. I know where we are. Todd Hill Road."

"Todd Hill," Anne says, drunk. "Make a right. I mean, left. Left turn, Louis." She points past Louis's face.

Louis says, "What are you going to do? You think they'll force you to go back with them?" Louis makes a right turn.

"I said *right* turn, Louis," Anne mumbles.

"What did Monty say to you at the D?" Louis asks.

"Monty told us about the new house," Anne says. "In Bel Air. Daddy said if *Sun City* does well, he's going to quote-unquote buy a football team."

"No pressure, no threats?" Louis asks, disappointed.

"Playing it smooth," Anne says.

Nathan is in the front seat, passed out, mumbling to himself.

"Did he say what team?" Louis asks. "I imagine since you've fucked most of the Raiders, negotiations will go smoothly."

"You're getting us lost again," Anne says in singsong.

"No," Louis says. "This is the way. Nathan knows, right, Nathan?"

Nathan sticks his head out the window and throws up, passes out again.

The music from the stereo plays, loud, the Replacements.

"How about Danielle?" Louis says. "Monty tells me she's going out with Tom Cruise."

"I doubt it," Anne says. "Monty loves to lie about shit like that."

"Tom Cruise is married to Nicole Kidman," I say.

"Monty also says that Danielle is now on a first-name basis with Macaulay Culkin," Louis says. "He says that Danielle refers to him as Mac."

This probably makes me feel drunker than I am.

"Let's get some blow," I say.

"Is she still your manager?" Louis asks me. "Danielle."

"I don't really understand what there is left to manage," Anne says. "Think about it, Louis. For once in your goddamn worthless life, think about it."

Louis passes me a flask, and I take a long sip. Sea Breeze. "Worthless seems to be the key word tonight."

"It seems to sum up a lot around here." Anne.

"What's this?" Louis asks.

"Your worthless life flashing before your eyes?"

Louis says, "Give me an hour alone in a room with you, Anne, and you wouldn't talk that way to me."

"Fuck you, Louis." Anne's hand grips my thigh as she steadies herself.

"What's this sign up here?" Louis says, straining his neck. He swerves into the oncoming lane, but there is no one else on this road for probably miles.

"Do you know where we're going?" Nathan moans from the front seat. "Because I don't know where we're going."

"I thought Nathan was asleep," Louis says.

"I *am* asleep," Nathan says. "I'm sleep-talking."

"Very common among people who dig worthless holes in the ground," Anne says.

"I know where we're going," Louis says.

"No, you don't," Anne says, then mutters, "Asshole."

"Anne," Louis yells. "Anne."

"What are you going to do, Louis?" Anne asks. "Stop the car and rape me?"

"What—you think Emery would stop it? You think Nathan would care?"

Anne sticks her finger in my mouth.

"I don't want to talk," Nathan says. "I'm too hot."

Anne lays her head in my lap.

"Louis," I say, speech garbled. "Get us home or let us out."

"Emery doesn't have any faith. I know *exactly* where we are."

"I *have* to piss," Nathan says.

"Five minutes," Louis says. "Hand me the flask."

I take another sip before handing it back to him.

"Emery," Louis says. "Prisoner."

Anne starts to sing something, then mumbles the rest, closes her eyes. She tries to make herself more comfortable.

"Is there any more beer?" Louis turns around. "Is Anne giving you head?"

"Eyes on the road, Louis," Anne says into my lap, handing him the bottle.

She turns her head up to look at me, plays with my chin. I brush her hand away.

Louis hands back the bottle. "Open this."

I twist off the cap and keep it.

"Drunk . . ." Nathan mutters.

Out the window trees move by quickly. We pass Todd Hill Road again.

Anne is kissing my legs, my thighs, drunkenly rubbing her face against them, saying things I can't hear. It is hot, even with the windows open, the wind blowing in. Louis downs the rest of the beer and tosses the bottle in the backseat. It hits Anne in the head.

Louis imitates Anne in a high voice: "Emery, what's going on?" and then, even higher: "Don't you like me anymore?"

I can hear Nathan opening the glove compartment. Anne takes my hand, puts my middle finger in her mouth. She is crying, her cheeks wet with tears, saliva.

"I don't think we should ever go back to the D ever," someone says.

Anne now has two of my fingers in her mouth. The night is pitch-black and smells good, like trees.

Louis turns right. Someone behind us flashes their brights and Louis pulls over.

"Hide the beer," Louis says. "Everyone shut up."

Mikey and Jeremiah and Monty and Danny get out of the car behind us. Nathan and Louis and I leave Anne asleep in the car.

"What's going on, Louie?" Monty says.

"If you call me Louie," Louis says, "I'll have to insist on calling you Minty."

"If I had this kind of land in Los Angeles County, anywhere in the area," Monty says, "I'd be a rich man."

"You *are* a rich man," Jeremiah mutters. "That's the only reason anyone talks to you."

Monty pats Jeremiah's back. "My son."

Louis walks over to some bushes to take a piss. Danny tries to videotape it but gives up because there's "no light."

Nathan fires at the water. BBs splash.

"I got one!" Nathan rocks the boat, excited. "I got one. This is it, man. They see their dead, floating down to the bottom and boom, their morale goes plummeting."

I lean back on one of the seats and listen to the water hit the sides of the boat.

"What time is it?" Nathan asks, looking at the sky.

Dark clouds move closer from behind the hills.

"Two conclusions: Becky's gross," Nathan says, struggling with the oars, "and Emery needs to plan an escape."

Nathan guides the boat to shore and steps out of it as I hand him the gun.

"It's already July," Nathan says. "I want to swim before it gets cold up here."

I sit up and play with the oars. Monty and Danielle come up the path from the house. Mikey is behind them, sunglasses on.

Monty sees me and waves. "Hold on. Let's take a ride in that thing."

Mikey holds the back of the boat steady, and Monty and Danielle climb in. Mikey gets in, too, and his weight almost sinks us. Mikey grabs the oars and starts moving us out onto the water. The clouds move closer, starting to block the sun.

"How about this?" Monty says. "I've never taken a meeting in a rowboat."

Danielle sits next to me to balance the weight. "This is how it should always be done. No phones, no interruptions."

"We need to talk," Monty says. "Seriously."

"Emery," Danielle says. "All personal shit aside, this is business."

Monty nods. "Closing this production is costing us a quarter million a day."

"It's been two weeks," Danielle says.

"You do the math, Emery," Monty says.

I hear a phone ring and Danielle pulls a cellular out of her purse. She talks quietly into it, then hangs up.

"We just want you to be reasonable," Danielle says. "I guess we have some . . . questions about your . . . progressive tendencies." Danielle tries to smile warmly.

I'm looking at my fingernails.

Monty's face gets red and he looks down. He starts talking in a quiet voice. "I don't want our relationship to sour here. I just want what's mine."

"We have a deal," Danielle says. "You made the deal and I arranged it. No one's going to benefit here."

Monty taps Mikey's shoulder, and Mikey stops rowing. The sky is only dark clouds. Mikey opens an umbrella and Danielle moves under it next to Monty. Raindrops, here and there, fall on the lake's surface.

"Are you trying to tell me that you have no intention of coming back and finishing this picture?" Monty asks.

"You're throwing everything away," Danielle says.

"They'll come after you." Monty again. "And I'll be there with them. Everything's going to go. House, money, production setup. All of it."

"Take it," I say, looking him in the eye. "I don't give a shit."

"What are you thinking? You think Warner Brothers is going to mistake bad manners for talent?"

The rain comes down a little harder now; soon my shirt is wet. No one says anything for quite a while. Monty takes out a cigarette and Mikey lights it for him.

"This isn't going to work," Danielle says. "No one's going to stand for this."

"You want more," Monty says, closer to a statement than a question.

"I want nothing," I say.

"No, I didn't ask you what you're going to end up with," Monty says. "I asked if you want more."

"More of what?" I ask. "More of this? More of you? More of her?"

"I'll do what I have to do, Emery," Monty says. "Whatever it takes."

"The man is offering you gross points," Danielle says.

"I'm not even sure Emery knows what that means," Monty says. "I'm not even sure he cares what gross points means."

"Gross points?" I ask after a minute. "Points that no one wants?"

"No," Danielle says quietly. "That's net."

"You're smart," Monty says admiringly. "Talking the philosophy of points and money while I'm telling you I'm willing to negotiate."

"He's willing to negotiate," Danielle tells me.

"You want someone off?" Monty says. "Is that it? Becky?

Gone if that's your choice. Briston? He's a little harder, but he's almost dead anyway. Gone."

"I don't care," I say, genuinely. "I really don't care."

"Oh, Emery, don't say that. You *do* care," Danielle says. "All that stuff you do for the Rain Forests and Rock Against Fur. Don't tell me you don't care."

"What do you want?" Monty asks.

"Tell us what you want," Danielle says.

"You're the picture," Monty says. "You are the picture."

My clothes are soaked to the skin. Monty flicks his cigarette into the lake, and Mikey lights another one for him. Monty looks at his cigarette. He takes a drag and flicks it into the lake.

"You've got what? Four scenes? Five left?" Monty.

"Five," Danielle says.

"Come back to L.A. Finish the picture, I'll get you the extras, and everyone's happy." Monty tries to smile. "Done deal?"

My sunglasses are on.

"Talk to him," Monty says to Danielle.

"Emery," Danielle says, putting her hand on my leg. "You could be five million on the Monday after this picture opens. Or . . ." Danielle pauses. "You could be the next Andrew McCarthy."

Monty taps Mikey. He starts rowing back to shore.

"Emery," Danielle says again, rubbing my leg.

"I'm not leaving," I say, "this . . . place."

Monty shakes his head, rubs his eyes. "One way or another."

The bottom of the boat has water in it. Mikey grunts as he rows.

It is too hot to do nothing but worse if you do something. Louis and I get up from the TV and go outside. Kevin the dog is lying in shade that the house provides. Kevin doesn't greet us; only his eyes move. Louis begins filling a wheelbarrow with dirt, while Nathan paces around the hole, muttering to himself.

"Do you see the way Becky fawns over Monty?" Louis says. "Becky lets him hold the baby."

"She lets everyone hold the baby," Nathan says. "She makes me hold it and I don't even want to."

Louis says, "I distance myself from that type of situation. That's what I'm doing here. I don't want to hang around the set, stay in the house in L.A., and have to see this kind of thing."

"I don't know why you're so upset," Nathan says. "She's the Actress."

"He's the Producer," Louis says. "Anne's the Rich Bitch. Emery's the Living Dead. So?"

"Monty's one of the biggest," Nathan says. "I mean the world, even."

"Nathan," Louis says in disbelief, "the man has Tourette's syndrome."

Nathan shovels more dirt into the wheelbarrow. "Pretty young actresses have certain relationships with big powerful producers."

"She doesn't have to fuck him," Louis says. "She doesn't have to fuck someone who actually enjoys parking in the studio's handicapped-only parking spaces."

Nathan lifts the wheelbarrow and moves it to the big pile of dirt.

"It's the nature of the job," Nathan says. "Have you ever thought that maybe Becky *has* fucked Monty? Whose kid do you think that is? Why else would she get the part, you moron? Because she's good?"

Louis looks at the ground, spits. "Creatures."

Wearing sunglasses, Becky and Anne come out the back door with Enzo and a plastic miniature swimming pool. They put the thing on the grass away from Nathan's hole, and Anne gets the hose. Becky takes off Enzo's clothes, and he runs around naked for a while, then stops to pee. Anne starts to fill up the baby pool, and Becky catches the kid and puts swim trunks on him. Makeup tries but cannot cover the bruises on Becky's leg, upper arm, neck. Becky's excuse this morning: She slipped in the shower. Over breakfast everyone laughed.

Nathan looks at them, rolls his eyes.

"Competition," Louis says to him. "Worried?"

"About that?" Nathan says. "Nah."

Anne and Becky take off their clothes, bikinis underneath. Becky looks covered with base. Becky lifts the kid into the water, careful not to splash herself. Danielle comes out of the house, wearing all white, carrying a beach chair. She sets it up, pulls a script out of her bag, sits down to read. She has a phone headset clipped on that she keeps slapping because of bad reception.

Soon Mikey comes outside.

"Mikey," Nathan says.

Mikey looks at us for a couple of seconds, then slowly walks over.

Nathan gets out of the hole and hands him a shovel.

"We need you," Nathan says. "We've got competition now."

Mikey takes off his jacket, undoes his tie, rolls up his sleeves. He says nothing as he hops into the hole. Nathan looks pleased.

"Where's Monty?" Becky asks, sitting Enzo in the pool.

"He's on the phone," Danielle says, after no one answers her.

Louis gives a look. Nathan shrugs.

"Date a salesgirl or something," Nathan says. "I don't know. I don't care."

Louis lowers his voice. "Salesgirls don't have bodies like this creature. Their bangability quotient isn't as high."

Danielle is watching me. She lowers her sunglasses and sort of smiles, then goes back to the script, making notes on it with a marker.

"I've got to talk to her," Louis says. "Make her understand."

Nathan says, "An ambitious actress is not good girlfriend material."

Louis hits his fist against his other palm. "Well, who the hell should I date?"

"Call up that town girl," Mikey says. "Hell."

"She likes *Emery*," Louis says. "They all like Emery, given the choice."

"Jesus," Mikey grunts, staring at Becky. "Look at those tits."

Louis shoots him an angry look. Mikey ignores it.

"Those tits, Mikey, are not biodegradable," Nathan says.

"Hey, neither is Emery's head," Louis says. "But he has a career, he has a Porsche, he dates Victoria's Secret models."

"Emery doesn't know how to drive," someone says.

Louis digs harder. "Look at it this way. If some crazed fan tries to shoot Emery in the head"—Louis pauses, breathes in, squints—"bullet'll bounce off."

Nathan looks up. "That should comfort you, Em."

I shrug, smell my fingers.

"Where the hell is Danny?" Nathan asks. "He should be here."

"Danny's at the lake," Louis says. "Filming."

"He's videotaping the *lake?*" Nathan says. "What is he? Demented?"

"No," Louis says. "USC film. Last night I saw him pointing the camera at the sky, trying to tape shooting stars."

Danielle looks at me again. Anne is lying in the baby pool, covering her eyes.

"Anne?" Nathan says. "Helping? Or did we have a little too much tequila in our OJ this morning?"

"I already have a swimming pool," Anne says.

"Yeah, but honey, you're drinking it," Nathan says.

Becky gets out of the water and pulls a packet of balloons from her bag. She fills one up with the hose, then squirts it on Enzo. He giggles, liking it.

The sound of an electric saw comes from inside the house, then hammering. Jeremiah.

"I don't understand everyone's priorities," Nathan says, pacing. "We have an opportunity to make things better, and everyone's too busy. They settle for *that.*" Nathan points accusingly at the kiddie pool. "All I need is a place to swim. That's all I need."

"And the occasional studio rewrite assignment." Louis

stops digging and gets a beer from the ice chest, glaring at Becky.

"I only need the pool," Nathan says.

Danielle kneels by the little pool and fills a water balloon with the hose and ties it. She turns around and walks with it behind her back, coming this way, headset still clipped on.

"Hot, Emery?" Danielle asks, balloon above her head now. "You look . . . uncomfortable."

"My anguish over the L.A. riots hasn't quite subsided," I say.

"Sure you don't need some cooling off?" Danielle says.

Anne sits up, lowers her sunglasses for a second, then puts them back on and lies down in the water. Danielle comes around to where I'm standing. "Come back."

When I back away, my foot slips and I fall into the hole, on my back. Danielle lifts the balloon over her head. I look up at her. "There's nothing to come back to."

Just before she lets the water balloon drop, Danielle says, "Finish the picture."

Danielle moves her hand down my neck to my bare chest, pulling away the sheet, down to my stomach and takes hold of my dick. Nathan is passed out drunk in the corner of the room, snoring. With her other hand Danielle starts taking off her clothes.

She's talking to me and I hear a few words, here and there. "Picture." "Relationship." "Necessary." "Budget." I look at the way her nose moves when she speaks. I'm not even beginning to get hard, but Danielle keeps stroking me and talking softly and I'm drunk and tired and I want to sleep.

The door to my room opens slowly and Danny is there, the camera pointed at us. Danielle doesn't see Danny and now she's touching her breasts, talking to them, and I'm watching her nose move and Danny's getting it on tape. Danny waves to me from behind the camera and I wave back. Danielle sees this and suddenly turns around and grabs the sheet off me. Danielle's face is red and she wraps the sheet around herself.

"Get out of here!" she yells at Danny. "Jesus, you ass-hole, *leave!*"

"Move over, Rob Lowe," Danny says, still taping. "It's the Emery Roberts Sex Tapes. Soon at your local video store."

I am naked on the bed and Danny points the camera at me. I cover myself with a pillow.

Nathan is still passed out, mumbles, "Pay or play . . ."

"Danny," I say.

Danny points the camera at Danielle, who is now throwing on her clothes. "And who's this mystery mistress? Don't worry, Danielle, we'll block out your face for the actual release."

"Come on, Danny," I say.

"No," Danielle says to me. "I'll leave, baby."

She grabs her shirt and storms out of the room, and I almost say something but don't.

"What's her problem?" Danny asks, zooming in on Nathan.

"Maybe your shitty . . . timing," I say.

"Did Danielle actually call her breast . . . Pumpkin?" Danny asks.

"I need sleep," I say.

"Real life's better," Danny says, getting his camera up again, hitting record, backing out of the room with it pointed at my face.

Louis throws a frozen pizza into the basket.

"How many of these do we need?" he asks.

"One," Danny says sarcastically. "We need one frozen pizza."

"I like these things," Louis says, throwing in another. "I like Wolfgang Puck ones better, but what do you expect in Vermont?"

"Don't be a snob," Danny says.

"Thank God there are some of us left," Louis says.

"I would like some Tic-Tacs," Danny says. "Where are the Tic-Tacs?"

"I could live in a Price Chopper. If they put in a TV and a toilet. Sent creatures to me at night." Louis.

Danny has the camera going, pointed at us. "Living in a supermarket. Remarkable idea."

"Actually Becky's place is bigger than this," Louis says. "Just not as . . . warm."

"Get vegetables, Danny," I say. "Because it's on the list."

"Perfect item for you to be concerned about," Louis mutters.

"Why do we have to shop?" Danny says. "Why doesn't Gladys do it?"

"She's taking care of Louis's son," I say.

"He's not *my* kid," Louis says. "I don't have any kids."

"At least that you know about," Danny says.

Louis throws in another frozen pizza box. "I am completely, adamantly prochoice."

"Those are awful," Danny says, zooming in on the refrigerated case. "They taste like people's feet."

A man in a red apron, a pen stuck behind his ear, comes down the aisle, snapping his fingers at Danny. "I'm sorry, but you're going to have to leave with the camera. Store policy."

"Why? The oranges don't want to be caught on film?" Louis asks. "The olive oil wants its privacy?"

"I thought it was only casinos that didn't allow photography," Danny says, pointing the camera at the man's face.

The man covers the lens with his hand and Danny puts the camera down.

Louis throws in a bottle of ketchup and a jar of pickles. "Vegetables," he says, glaring at me.

Danny reads the *Weekly World News* headline. "Elvis was my mother."

"Elvis was *my* mother," Louis says. "He was Mikey's mother, too."

Still hovering, the man in the red apron recognizes me, does a double take. "You're Emery Roberts."

"He's Elvis's mother," Louis says.

"I really love your movies," the man says, lighting up, grabbing a milk carton. "Do you think I could get your autograph? Make it to Brian. I really liked you in *Top Gun.*"

He hands me the milk carton and a pen. I sign my name.

"I'm Brian Cooper," he says. "Manager here. Go ahead with your camera work, if you want. Just keep it low-key."

"Low-key," Danny promises.

"Are you shooting some sort of movie or something?" the guy asks.

"Documentary," Danny says, pointing the camera at him. "For Showtime."

The man nods, smiles, looks into the camera lens. "Uh-huh."

"Well, thank you, Mr. Cooper," Louis says, shaking his hand. "Thank you so much."

"Let me know if you need anything," Mr. Cooper says,

looking at my autograph on the carton. He walks away, down an aisle.

"Mr. Cooper really liked you in *Top Gun*," Louis says, looking over the list. "Too bad you weren't in it."

Danny takes the newspaper from me and flips through the pages until he finds the one he wants. Danny says, "This is it. 'Film star Emery Roberts believed captured by UFO.'"

"Unidentified Flying Ovitz," Louis says.

Nathan reads on. "Aliens want him for their own feature film production studio on planet seven light-years from earth."

"What kind of contract did they offer?" Louis asks.

Danny throws the paper in the cart. "Did you get Häagen-Dazs?"

"We need Sea Breeze fixin's," Louis says. "Top priority."

"Get chicken," Danny says. "And see if there's any arugula or tahini. What's in a Sea Breeze?"

"It's like you ask God to spit in a glass," Louis says, absently, looking over the list.

"I think you can get God's spit on aisle seven," Danny says.

Danny puts the camera on a shelf, facing outward. He and Louis move into frame and stare at the camera; then Danny puts it on his shoulder again, focuses.

Louis says, "Maybe we should get some stuff for the pool. Like chlorine . . . or battery acid . . . or something."

"Let's not get ahead of ourselves," Danny says. "Let's try to break that habit."

"I don't think you need to offer that advice to Emery," Louis says.

"We have to get back soon," Danny says. "I promised Nathan I'd work."

"Get Monty to dig," Louis says. "Get Danielle."

"They left," Danny says, zooming in for my reaction.

"They're gone?" I ask.

"No joke," Danny says. "They took a flight from Albany this morning."

"Get champagne," Louis says. "Celebration time."

"They left Mikey to watch you," Danny says.

Louis says, "So get domestic champagne."

Dinner's in front of the TV, all of us except Jeremiah, who is still trying to fix the electricity. The lights in the room flicker, but the TV doesn't and we watch something I wasn't in on tape. Anne sits next to me, drinking Absolut from a large glass, no ice. Mikey is in the corner of the room, asleep.

Anne mutters, "Monty can pick them."

"Do you think the Corleones had a pool at that house?" Nathan asks. "I mean, do Mafia people swim?"

"Aren't you glad they're gone?" Anne sort of whispers to me.

"Shh," Danny says, pointing the camera at the TV.

The lights start to flicker, brown out.

Louis says, "Shit, what's happening here?"

The room goes pitch-black and Enzo starts to wail.

"Jesus," Danny says.

Anne's hand is on my leg. Everyone is moving around. Jeremiah has a candle.

"Sorry to ruin the movie," Jeremiah says. "I'm trying to fix things."

Louis looks at me. I can barely make out his face in the half-lit room.

"Sea Breeze?" Louis suggests. "Dynamo?"

Anne groans and runs her fingers through my hair. "It's raining, Louis."

"Danny's already committed," Louis says. "Right, Danny?"

"Right."

Louis reaches out his hand; he pulls me up from the couch.

"Come on," Louis says. "Anne?"

"Pass," she says.

"What are you going to do, dollface?" Louis asks. "Liquor cabinet's sucked dry. Going to distill your own?"

"No," Anne says. "I'm going to debate on which blunt object I'm going to bludgeon you to death with when you get home."

"Emery? The D?" Louis says. "Guaranteed to get that bad taste of Monty and Danielle out of your mouth."

"Or his money back?" Anne asks.

We drive down to the D and Louis gets Sea Breezes and Danny videotapes himself playing Triv Whiz. The pool table has a bucket on the felt, catching a leak in the ceiling. We play around it and Louis beats me three games in a row.

Louis and I are in the wall room, the tape deck blaring House of Pain. Raining outside, hot everywhere. I slap a mosquito on my arm. I smell like Marlboros. Someone has painted on the wall

abe vigoda is alive and well and LIVING with jim morrison on 13th street between 3rd and 4th

Louis stirs a can of blue paint and brings the brush out to look at it, testing for color. He mixes in red.

"Learned this from Barbara Lazaroff," Louis says. "If there's one thing the woman taught me, it was that there are a million different shades of color."

"Blue is blue," I say.

"That's what I said," Louis says. "But we're wrong. There's red blue and there's green blue. I think it's called teal. Then there's blue with yellow. A million different shades."

"Blue is just blue," I say.

Louis finishes mixing in the red and brings the brush up to look at the new color. The paint drips down his hand, his arm, some of it onto his jeans. I look out the open window, at rain coming down. I wipe sweat off my forehead.

"When you did that plane crash movie," Louis says, "did you shoot in Alaska? The story takes place in Alaska, right?"

"All I remember is that there were a lot of Canadians around," I say, staring outside. "So it must have been . . . Canada."

"I want to go to Alaska," Louis says, painting a big blue circle on the wall.

Outside, it pours and Nathan is at the pool site, wearing only shorts, drenched, digging mud out of the hole.

Nathan looks up and squints in the rain. "Get Louis down here," he calls up.

"What's up?" Louis sticks his head out the window.

"You," Nathan yells. "Come on here and help."

"It's raining," Louis says.

"Master of the obvious," Nathan mutters loudly.

"It's just mud," Louis says from inside. "You're dealing with mud, Nathan."

"This is a confusing, unrewarding business, shit-for-brains," Nathan yells. "So be considerate."

"Wait until it stops raining," Louis yells down. "You're not getting anything done. You're not getting anywhere."

Nathan throws down the shovel and starts to walk to the house.

Louis resumes painting. He fills the blue circle with more blue. I light a cigarette.

"Jeremiah sees you," Louis says, "there's going to be a fight."

I take another drag, looking at the smoke float in front of me.

"Rule number one," Nathan says, coming into the room and looking at me. "Emery's breaking rule number one."

"Nobody likes a tattletale," Louis says, painting a shark's fin, in black, in the center of the blue circle. The paint smears and drips.

"It's never going to get done," Nathan says. "The pool will never be done."

Becky, wearing sunglasses, comes in with the baby, sets him down, hands him a crayon to play with. Becky sniffs the air and sees the cigarette in my hand.

Becky says, shaking her finger, "Bad Emery."

I take another drag and flick the cigarette out the window.

"Prove it," Louis says. "Prove Emery smoked in the house."

Nathan takes a red marker and draws a huge cigarette on the wall, a circle around it and a slash through the middle.

"Did Monty say anything to you?" Becky asks.

I shake my head.

"So you don't know what Monty's going to do? What Monty's planning?"

"Did he want you back there?" Nathan asks, drawing a turtle with big sharp teeth.

"He said I should just stay," Becky says. "Monty said I should just stay put."

"My stomach starts to hurt," Louis says, "every time you mention that slimeball's name."

"Hey, I'm writing a screenplay," Becky interrupts. "In the meantime."

"About?" Nathan asks uninterestedly.

Louis glowers, studies the paint.

"It's a love story," Becky says. "Set in Ireland. During the Irish potato famine that happened."

No one says anything.

"I haven't really got it all worked out yet," Becky says. "But Googie and Huggie said they'd help me out if I needed it."

"Googie and Huggie?" Louis asks. "Oh, Christ."

"They're the writers, the auteurs on *Sun City*," Nathan scowls.

"Googie and Huggie wrote it?" Louis asks. "I thought Nathan penned that masterpiece."

"They're just assigned to rewrite it," Becky says. "Nathan wrote it. But Nathan is—Monty's word—dead."

Anne comes in and sits next to me.

"Someone's been smoking," Anne says. "Very dangerous given Jeremiah's current state of mind."

"Where is the Gentle Giant?" someone asks.

"Danny's videotaping him putting in some tiles," Anne says. "But he's got a nose for smoke."

Nathan finishes drawing a gun, pointed at the red turtle, and is now doing bullets, coming at it, rapid fire.

From below the phone rings, someone answers it. Mikey sticks his head in the doorway. "Emery," Mikey says. "Telephone. It's Mr. Factor."

Anne sighs. "Doesn't he ever give up?"

"What should I tell him?" Mikey asks.

"Tell him that Emery left," Louis says. "Tell him that Emery cannot deal with Monty's thinly disguised loathsomeness."

"He knows you're here," Mikey says to me.

"Tell him Emery's in a meeting." Louis.

"I'm in a meeting," I repeat.

"Tell him that Joel Silver's up here and Emery's meeting with him about possibly playing Bruce Willis's sidekick in *Hudson Hawk 2*." Louis grins.

"Shall I tell him you'll call him later?" Mikey asks me.

I shrug. Mikey leaves.

"What's the big deal?" Becky asks.

*   *   *

"It's all I can think about," Nathan says.

The sun has set and it's still getting dark out and we're all watching the last of the fireworks display that the city of Suzanna is putting on for its two hundredth anniversary. The finale isn't much: Six big rockets explode at once, colors, booms echoing out over the valley a second or two later. In the warm night, heads are cocked up to the sky, and bugs are everywhere in swarms. A cloud of smoke begins to drift toward the hills, and you can smell it.

"Relax, Nathan," Louis says. "What's all you can think about?"

Nathan and Louis and I stand apart from the others. Louis tries to light a joint, but his matches are wet from sitting in the kiddie pool.

"It," Nathan says, looking at me as if I were crazy. "The hole. The pool over there."

"Hear from Danielle?" Louis asks. "Speaking of holes."

I shake my head and hand Louis dry matches.

"Mikey told me about Monty's next movie," Nathan says. "Mikey's friends with the screenwriter. Idiot I know back in L.A. Jane Walton."

"I don't want to talk about it," Louis says.

He lights the joint and hits off it.

Nathan is fidgeting, keeps looking at the hole. Louis

hands him the joint and Nathan hits off it, then passes it to me and I do, too.

"Listen," Nathan says, exhaling. "It's called *The Vegetarians*, and it's about this band of renegade vegetarians, the Animal Liberation Front. They live in a futuristic society that requires the consumption of animal flesh."

"Make the vegetarians into talking mice," Louis says, "and you've got a lucrative deal with Amblin."

Nathan keeps talking. "They have these Meat Police. They're the ones who crack down on *non*meat eaters. These outlaws live up in the hills and eat berries and dirt, and every so often they go on these vigilante missions, freeing cows and pigs from slaughterhouses."

I hit off the joint again, and Louis takes it from me and smokes.

"I couldn't believe it," Nathan says. "I mean this Jane girl, who wrote it. That's the kind of creature you want to avoid, with thoughts like that."

"Vegetarian heroes." Louis makes a face.

"She's an idiot." Nathan sighs. "Let's not go to the movie when it comes out."

"Beware of what only eats vegetables," Louis says.

"Well, that rules out half the girls in Hollywood who've gone down on Emery," Nathan says.

"I wish I could challenge her to a Roman Candle War," Louis says. "Crazy vegetarian-eating bitch."

"You've got fireworks?" Nathan asks.

"A whole box," Louis says. "I got too drunk on the Fourth to use them."

Nathan points to the hole. "I'm going to do it. If it takes me the rest of my fucking life."

"Genius or psychotic asshole," Louis says. "Emery? Which?"

"What's a Roman Candle War?" I ask Louis, who is too stoned to answer at this moment.

Nathan is high, too. "Sounds serious."

Danny sets up his camera on a tripod while he shares a joint with Anne. After a big hit Anne exhales. She sits down, then goes flat on her back, tapping her feet on the ground. Louis comes out a few minutes later and rounds us all up near the camera and tells us about the Roman Candle War.

"You stand twenty paces apart," Louis explains, holding an armful of long fireworks. "Only rule is, you have to aim for the head."

People kind of laugh, but Louis is serious. I'm high and watching Anne, her face barely visible in this dark.

"To sort of settle the tensions around here," Louis says, "I'm going to have Emery and Jeremiah go first."

"No way," Jeremiah says. "No one's going to fire at me."

"Anne, you're part of the same family," Louis says. "We need a little catharsis here. We need to all make friends again, and everyone's got to stop blaming my boy Emery here for stuff beyond his control."

Jeremiah rolls his eyes. "Emery agreeing to three million to star in a movie about a group of Colombian computer hackers is 'beyond his control'?"

Danny pulls a joint out of his back pocket and lights it, then hands it to me.

"This is good stuff," Danny says, checking the settings on his camera.

"I can never tell the difference," Louis says. "Good drugs, bad drugs."

Jeremiah points to Anne, who stares at Louis, high. "Anne could never tell the difference either."

"Friend of mine brought that stuff in from Jamaica," Danny says, pointing at the joint, unable to focus on it.

Jeremiah hits, then hands it back. "Don't count on it."

Danny puts the lit end in his mouth, extinguishes it, and places it back in his pocket. "I've got to stay normal. I've got to get this war Louis is having on film."

"Tape," Anne corrects.

"Get me some pot," I say. "I think I'll start smoking a lot."

Danny says, "Get it yourself."

"I remind you that you're talking to Emery Roberts," Anne says. "The phrase 'get it yourself' means nothing to him."

"Emery's motto," Jeremiah says. "Vacuous and Proud of It."

Danny says, not listening, "I'll work on it."

Jeremiah looks at the camera. "Can you tape in the dark like this?"

Danny doesn't say anything, scratches his head thoughtfully. He shrugs. Anne is smiling, high from the pot.

"Ready?" Louis asks. "Anne? Emery?"

Jeremiah sits down, plays with Enzo.

Louis puts a Roman candle in my hand and one in Anne's.

"Rule is?" Anne says, high.

Louis speaks slowly. "You have to aim for the *head*."

Louis sets us up, back to back, and we walk twenty paces apart and turn around to face each other across the backyard, a lantern from the porch the only illumination. Louis runs over and hands me a pack of matches from Chaya Brasserie and runs to Anne, gives her a lighter.

"Aim for the *head*," Louis says, shouting so everyone will listen.

The others back away. Louis lets out a high, excited laugh.

"Gentlemen," Louis says, "light your fuses."

Louis runs away from Anne, who lights her stick. I fumble with the matches, manage to light one, bring it to my fuse. When I look up, an orange fireball zooms toward me. I dodge, and another one flies, this time blue, higher—sounds like *foomp*. One comes out of my Roman candle but only hits the ground. I aim in Anne's direction, but it's hard to see in the darkness. Another fireball flies from mine. One of Anne's falls toward me. I duck; it misses. Finding the silhouette of Anne's white shirt, I aim. Her fireballs sail over my head now, and *foomp*, one comes from mine. It flies across the length of the yard and hits her in the chest. A red fireball stays there, pulsing for a couple of seconds, and Anne screams. She swats the ball away and drops her candle.

"Emery wins," Louis says. "Isn't that better? Don't we all feel better?"

A last blue fireball shoots out of Anne's candle, bounces along the surface of the grass before going out. Anne just sits on the grass, looking down the front of her shirt, a big burn hole through her left breast pocket.

"I'm hit," Anne says.

Louis says, "Dangerous game."

"I'm scarred for life," she mutters drunkenly. "A mutant. What man is going to love me now? How am I going to get a decent husband?" She is crying, hysterical.

"Jesus, Jeremiah," someone says. "Get her to Austin Riggs."

Louis, ignoring Anne, has already set up another opponent for me, Mikey.

Anne stumbles up to the house, everyone too stoned to help, and walks in the back door, still looking down at her shirt, sobbing.

Mikey and I square off at twenty paces, light the fuses, and aim. I wait for my candle to get going, but nothing happens. Mikey's fireballs fly, one after another, straight toward me. I look down at my Roman candle again, tapping it against my leg, but nothing. When I look up again, a fireball hurtles toward me and hits me in the chest, then bounces off.

Louis yells, "Emery is unseated after just his first win. Mikey is now champion of the world."

I brush off my shirt and sit next to Jeremiah and Enzo. Becky and Nathan and Mikey and Louis all hold lit Roman candles, two or three each, and it's a free-for-all. It seems like hundreds of bright fireballs are going, in every direction. Sulfur smoke, green of the trees, heat. Danny is filming, panning the camera left and right.

"Can I stay?" I ask Jeremiah.

Jeremiah lifts the baby and looks at its face. "I don't think you're capable of doing anything but."

Upstairs I stand in front of Anne's door, rubbing my eyes for a minute.

"Yes?" I hear her say.

I push the door open and step in. She sees me and laughs, her face puffy from crying.

"What?" she says. "You want some of this?"

Anne holds out a half-smoked joint, still lit. I shake my head, looking at her feet.

"Nice feet," I say.

"I'm glad you realize that relationships require some approximation of honesty, of viable communication, baby."

She shuts the door and puts the joint out in an ashtray, waves her hand in the air to clear the smoke. In front of the window, fireballs fly.

"Why'd you stop?" Anne asks. "I mean, with us."

She turns around to face me. I'm looking at her feet again, dazed, strung-out. I light a cigarette and flip through a magazine on the desk. I come to a page with a picture of me on it. I am standing on my head at the beach and there are two girls in bikinis holding my legs up.

"What are you going to do?" Anne asks. "What are we going to do?"

I sort of shrug.

"I miss you," Anne says.

"Me, too," I say, shutting the magazine. "I miss myself, too."

She takes my hand and turns off the lights. We sit on the bed.

"I didn't mean to, you know," Anne says. "I understand why you went with Danielle."

I look out the window. A green fireball passes, lights up the room for just a second. In that flash Anne kisses me quickly.

She starts to unbutton my shirt while kissing my neck.

"Please," Anne says, almost a whisper. "Please, Emery," and then, softer: "You're the only one I trust."

She pulls off her T-shirt, her hands are on me. It's hard to keep my eyes open.

ACT III

It is pouring rain. Nathan is in the kitchen. Louis stares out the window at the hole in the ground.

Nathan says, "I can't let this happen."

"It's just water," Louis says. "A pool needs water, so lighten up."

"It's not just water," Nathan shouts. "It's acid rain, and soon the whole thing's going to fill up. We have to cover it."

"You'll get killed," Louis says, stretching. "You'll be struck by lightning. Actually not a bad idea considering all the good times we're having."

Nathan looks around the kitchen, searching through drawers and cupboards. He finally finds some plastic garbage bags and rips open a box.

"What are you doing?" Louis asks. "Getting rid of Emery? I have to tell you, pal, that if it weren't for Mikey, no one would notice."

"In baseball," Nathan says, "when there's a rainout, to protect the field, they cover it in plastic."

"That's huge plastic," Louis says, opening a beer. "What are you going to do with those? Sew them together?"

Nathan finds tape in the top drawer and begins to tape one trash bag, side by side, next to another, making a big blanket of trash bags, Scotch-taped together.

Louis shakes his head. "Oh, no. We've lost him."

Becky comes in.

"Where's Enzo?" one of us asks after a long, protracted silence.

"He's asleep," Becky says, heading toward the refrigerator. "The little monster."

There's a rumbling sound, but it's not thunder. Nathan moves to the window.

"What is it?" Becky asks. "What's going on?"

"Nathan," Louis pleads. "Give it up. Nature's going to win."

The roar and rumble get louder. It sounds like engines.

Louis says, "Townies are coming to kill us. Where's Mikey?"

Nathan, looking out the window, says, "Worse."

"What?" Becky asks in a voice that suggests she knows what.

"Monty," Louis says, standing behind Nathan.

Becky runs out of the room.

On the front driveway Monty steps out of a big white car. Trucks roll in behind him, three, four, five of them. They park on the front lawn, and the big ones, eighteen-wheelers, line up on the side of the driveway. Men jump out, opening doors.

Monty takes his time walking into the house, an assistant holding an umbrella over him.

In the front hall Monty and Jeremiah begin arguing. Monty spots me and ushers Jeremiah into a room off the hall, shutting the door behind them. Dmitri, the first AD, shakes water off his umbrella.

"Emery," Dmitri says, heavy accent. "So nice to see you."

"Unbridled sarcasm. Lovely." Louis comes up behind me. Becky is already talking to one of the men in the trucks.

"Ah, Louis," Dmitri says. "Have you found a job yet? William Morris, I hear, offered you something in the mailroom. Can you verify?"

Louis guzzles the rest of the beer, glares at Dmitri.

Jeremiah and Monty come out of the room, and Jeremiah looks at me, shrugs, resigned. He reaches into my shirt pocket, pulls out a cigarette, and lights it, inhaling deeply.

"It's your house," Louis mutters.

Jeremiah shows me the check Monty gave him.

"I can't say no to a hundred," Jeremiah says. "I can say no to a lot of things, but not this. I just can't say no to a hundred."

"Mohammed won't come to the mountain," Monty says from down the hall. "You know what happens then?"

"Who the fuck's Mohammed?" Louis says.

* * *

Nathan works on the pool and Danny videotapes. The rain has left the hole half full of water, and Nathan scoops up mud and sludge and throws it over the side.

The crew sets up trailers. Cars seem to come and go all day. People are everywhere. A white limousine pulls up, and Hurley and Briston and Danielle step out. They see me but don't say anything as they go into the house.

Louis comes out the back door and helps Nathan for a while. They hardly make a dent after a couple of hours, and Louis finally throws his bucket as far as he can into the bushes.

"What's wrong?" Nathan asks.

Louis looks at me and rolls his eyes.

Nathan says, "We're getting it. Come on."

Danny points the camera at Louis and zooms in, plays with the focus.

"Becky's inside right now," Danny says. "Rehearsing."

"How boring," Louis says.

"A love scene," Danny says.

"Boring, boring," Louis says.

"Hurley and Becky are doing their lines and they have to kiss at the end and she's supposed to be the one hot for him, right? So they kiss and Louis is looking at them kiss and then Becky sticks her *tongue* in Hurley's mouth," Danny says.

"Boring, boring, boring." Louis scoops up more mud, water into a bucket, then throws it over the side of the hole.

"Her *tongue*," Danny says. "You know, Louis, she doesn't have to do that."

"Actress," Nathan says. "You go out with an actress."

"What about you and that townie chick?" Danny asks.

"Different," Louis mutters, unable to speak clearly because of the exertion.

"What does that make you?" Nathan asks.

"Don't get preachy, asshole," Louis says. "Nathan's always getting preachy about something. About townie chicks. Pools. Screenplays. Jesus, you never shut up."

Mikey comes over. "Monty wants to see you."

"He's busy," Louis says.

Mikey says, "I don't want to have to carry you."

Walking away from the hole, I hear Nathan mutter, "Emery shouldn't give in so easily like that."

Mikey follows me into the house, where Monty and Danielle and Briston and Hurley are sitting on a couch that wasn't here yesterday. I sit in a chair facing them. There are two men putting in more phone lines, and once I'm seated, Monty waves for them to leave the room.

"Time to talk," Monty says.

Mikey stands by the doorway to let no one in.

"Emery," Danielle says.

"No," I say.

Briston lights a pipe. Hurley glares at me.

"Emery," Monty says. "You have to realize that this isn't done."

"This is not done," Danielle says.

"We don't haul two hundred-some-odd people up to the middle of nowhere every day," Monty says calmly. "We've got two weeks left on this thing. Twenty little pages."

"Which I might add, Googie and Huggie are working on right now," Briston hisses.

"You think you're going to walk away from this with what? A slap on the wrist?" Monty.

Hurley says, "Your little stunt's already cost everyone a lot of time and money."

"Why does Hurley talk like a TV show?" I ask.

Hurley laughs, disgustedly. Briston puts a hand on Hurley's arm.

"You little fucker," Briston mutters.

"Could Emery and I be alone?" Monty says. "This meeting would run a lot smoother if we were left alone."

"This whole thing would run a lot smoother if the spoiled little shit . . ." Hurley starts.

"*Leave,*" Monty bellows.

Danielle and Hurley and Briston leave. Monty pats the cushion next to him, and I get up, tired, and sit by him.

"Emery," Monty says. "I'm not asking you to put on a bunny suit. I'm asking that you finish your five scenes. And then you can go on with . . . your life."

"I don't want to, Monty," I say.

Monty's face loses all forced friendliness, and he flips through some papers on the coffee table.

"Monty," I say.

"Listen," he says, pointing his finger in my face. "I told them I would get you to finish and you're going to finish."

"What if I don't?" I say.

"Then my friend Mikey over there is going to take you into the middle of these woods out here somewhere and put a bullet in your heart, you loathsome little bastard."

"I'll do it," I say. "Fine. Whatever."

"Ten days," Monty says.

I get up and Mikey looks at me.

"What in the fuck are you looking at?" I ask.

"Nothing," Monty says. "He's not looking at anything."

Mikey smiles.

"If you're in the middle of an ocean," Monty says, "and you're holding on to a life raft, you can't ask yourself, 'Do I love this life raft?' Truth is you *have* to love it. Hugging this life raft isn't something you *consider*. You've got no choice."

"I've always known that, Monty," I say.

Outside, Nathan hands Louis a bucket. Danny aims the camera at me.

"He's doing it," Danny says. "I can tell he's doing it."

"That's it?" Louis asks. "Just like that? They win?"

Danny says, shutting off the camera, "Monty always wins."

"Jeremiah's pissed?" Louis asks.

Nathan shakes his head. "Location fees have a way of persuading people."

"This isn't good," Louis says, looking at the hole. "I mean, what if they ran studios like this?"

"They do," Nathan says. "And who's *they?*"

"They," Louis says, spitting. "Them."

I'm sitting in my trailer with Louis and Anne, watching TV. Anne and I play gin, but I don't really know the rules and I'm not paying attention.

"Never been in a trailer this nice," Louis says. "What's that? Espresso machine?"

"It's in the contract," Anne says. "Nice is in the contract."

Anne lays down her cards and, relieved, so do I. She wins.

"Are you done for the day?" Louis asks.

"The grips they hired up here don't know what they're doing, Monty says. It's taking forever to set up simple stuff." Anne stands up, stretches.

Someone knocks on the door. When Louis heads over to answer it, I motion for him to wait. When whoever it is knocks again, then a third time, I let Louis open the door: Briston wearing a Dodgers cap and a Will Rogers Never Met Monty Factor T-shirt.

"May this trailer be safe from tigers," Briston says, stepping inside, brushing past Louis.

"Why's Briston always saying that?" Louis asks. "Why's Briston always blessing the fucking trailer? That's like the fourth fucking time."

"Simply because it fucking works, my dear young man," Briston says. "Has this trailer been attacked by tigers?"

Louis looks confused, shakes his head. "Talentless English has-beens perhaps, but no, not tigers."

"It works." Briston shrugs. "Is it true that the Hollywood Agents Association has found you unequivocally unfit for active duty and that you are currently seeking employment at the Suzanna Suicide Hotline Center?"

"You worry too much, Briston," Louis says.

Anne pours vodka into a big glass from a small bottle of Absolut she now carries around with her everywhere.

Briston says, "Ninety percent of the things I worry about *never* happen."

"Never mind," Anne says.

"I've had a chance to look at Friday's rushes," Briston says.

"Any good?" someone asks.

"I liked them best, Monty liked them second best, and Hurley thought they were shit." Briston puts a pipe in his mouth but doesn't light it. "I told Monty let's not reshoot. Not that I care, but Emery should find this pleasant news."

"Let's *not*," I say.

"Or we'll never get the bloody thing finished, now will we?" Briston asks politely.

"Sooner the better," Anne mutters.

Briston says, "Anyway, these fools won't be ready until tomorrow with the newly, brilliantly devised tree scene, so today's a wrap for you, my little nonentity." Briston pauses. "I've come to the conclusion that given our hair-raisingly moronic script, only ninety seconds of this movie actually work. But I'm confident that it will open big. And build."

"It'll rain tomorrow," Louis says. "It's saying so on the news."

"It rains when I say it rains." Briston bristles. "Weather is a whim, a fancy. It all happens the way I want it to. Weather suits me and my schedule. Not the other way around."

"Briston, I'm glad you'll be dead by the time I get back to work so I'll never have to deal with you on any level," Louis says.

"Dear boy," Briston says. "The only work you're ever going to get is perhaps male hooker, and considering the rumors circulating about your privates, even *that's* an iffy prospect."

Louis goes back to watching TV. Briston leaves. Anne starts to deal another hand.

"I'm going into town," Louis says. "I need food. I need a cheeseburger."

"There's an AA meeting at five," Anne says.

"Monty's after *you* not to drink," Louis points out. "Not Louis, dear creature."

"Humor *me*," Anne says after a long swallow of vodka.

Louis switches off the TV, stands up.

Louis says, "Fashionably sober people. The dregs."

"Monty's got a shrink on the payroll," Anne says. "His hours are booked through next week. Where does that leave you?"

Louis says, "I guess that leaves Sea Breeze as my best option."

Monty knocks on the table, checks the bet.

"Emery," Louis says. "Bet."

I am holding aces and eights and toss three dollars into the pot.

"Three," Briston says. "And I'm afraid I'm going to have to raise three."

Jeremiah scratches his chin and lights a cigarette. "Fold. I keep up like this, I'll lose the whole thing, Monty."

"You want real thrills," Monty says, studying his cards. "Take the money you get from this picture, we'll drive to

Atlantic City tonight and put it all on the hard ten or hard way four."

"He hasn't the balls," Briston says. "Hurley's bet."

Hurley is completely wasted drunk, his head thrown back, asleep. Briston takes the cards out of his hands and puts them on the table.

"Hurley folds," Briston says. "Makeup will not be happy tomorrow. Hurley, wake up. I demand it." Hurley doesn't. "Hurley is eating too much. He looks heavy in the rushes. I do believe Hurley is one pizza away from getting his fat ass kicked off this film."

"What is that . . . *thing?*" Louis points his cards toward Hurley.

Monty closely examines Hurley's nose. "That, you little failure, is a movie star."

"He smells like a dead cat," Louis says. "Actors are disgusting."

"This movie doesn't require actors," Monty says carefully. "It requires movie stars."

"Hurley can't talk, let alone act or in any way be human, yet he's become very popular by simulating these talents." Briston eyes his cards warily.

Jeremiah shudders. "Shit, that'd be money. Putting it all on the hard ten and *hitting*."

Louis says, impatient, "Briston raises. It's six to you, Nathan."

Nathan throws in his money. "Monty," Nathan says. "You think you could get some of these truck drivers to help out with the digging?"

"Teamsters," Monty says. "You're lucky if they don't make you serve them fucking breakfast in bed."

"Everyone even?" Louis asks. "I'm in."

Monty snaps his fingers, trying to remember something. "Dustin says that, doesn't he? In—what was that picture called?"

"Did anyone hear about Charlie Sheen paying ninety-three thousand dollars for a baseball?" someone asks.

"Charlie has *earned* the right to pay ninety-three thousand dollars for a baseball," someone answers.

"Everyone's in," Louis says. "Show."

Cards are turned over.

"Emery's got the high hand," Louis says. "Aces and eights."

"That's three hands in a row," Monty says. "I'm quitting while I still have my fortune."

"Aces and eights," Louis says. "Buffalo Bill was shot holding that hand."

"Wild Bill Hickok," Briston says, counting up his money, separating blue chips from red from white. "Twit."

"Twit?" Louis glares at Briston. "What kind of an insult is that? Like calling someone a ninny."

Louis counts up my money. Jeremiah starts to deal another hand.

"Anaconda," Jeremiah says. "Hooks are wild. Three, two, one to the left. Roll seven. Emery? Getting all this?"

"Anyone to the D?" Louis asks the table. "Emery, what's your per diem?"

"Emery has to work early tomorrow," Briston whispers, leaning in.

"Big deal. We'll be *back* early tomorrow," Louis whispers back.

"May I remind everyone that it *is* early tomorrow." Monty yawns.

"You want to find women?" Briston asks. "Is that it? You animal."

Louis thumps his fist against his other palm. "Creatures."

"What about Ms. Becky Sawyer?" Briston asks, glancing over at Monty. "A slightly used but suitable creature."

"What does that mean?" Louis asks threateningly. "You limey fag."

"Does Louis have a house pass?" Briston asks Monty. "Because if he does, I want to see it."

"What are you two yakking about?" Monty asks. "Planning your escape, Emery?"

"I'm yours," I say.

"I always like to hear that." Monty smiles. "Damn, it sounds good."

"Emery has morals," Nathan says.

"Emery declined to star in *She's Having a Baby*," Briston says. "You don't have to justify Emery to me, dear Nate."

"That's *Nathan*," Nathan says. "How long do you have to live, Briston? I hear it's a matter of weeks."

"Monty," Briston says. "I need you to talk to Googie and Huggie about the pages I received today. Totally unsatisfactory."

"Go easy on them, old man," Monty says. "Briston's pissed about the Writers Guild arbitration. No writing credit for the Brister."

"I am king," Briston says. "They'll do my bidding and do it well, or off with their heads."

Nathan asks the room, "Does the room want to know why I gave up screenwriting?"

"Let me guess," Briston says. "Because you're a dime a dozen? What was that last script of yours I read, Nate? *Cement Dog? Cement Geek?* Something *Cement*. It was savagely hilarious. It took risks. It boiled with energy. It even managed to shock. *Quest for Fire* had more dialogue. What studio has it? Turnaround Pictures?"

Hurley mumbles something, then leans over to his side and starts drooling, crying in his sleep for someone named Ragmop.

"You better stop looking around like you don't know where you are," Briston warns me.

"Briston," I say. "Please, please leave me the fuck alone."

Briston says, "I do believe we have discovered a new archetype: the whining zombie."

"I do believe I fold," Jeremiah says.

Outside, it rains. Nathan stands in front of a washing machine in the Laundromat in town, reading instructions. Louis stares at him, dumbfounded.

"Trouble?" Louis asks.

"No trouble," Nathan says. "I've just never, like, done this before."

"Why not let someone on the crew take care of it?" Louis asks. "Emery can get you a laundry clause."

"It took us over an hour to get change for a fifty in this pathetic little town," Nathan grumbles. "I'm not *not* going to use these quarters."

Danny is videotaping a girl who's folding shirts, three machines down from us. The girl keeps looking over, smiling.

"Rain's got to stop," Louis says. "It can't go on like this forever."

Nathan continues to read the instructions on the machine.

"If Monty would be cool enough to lend me thirty or forty guys in the crew," Nathan says, "we'd have that pool done in a day or two."

Louis says, "It really is way too hot in this state. They should do something about it. It's insane."

I say, "Just put in . . . some soap." I swallow twice. "Please."

"I want to get it right," Nathan says.

Danny follows the girl with the camera as she walks over to me. The girl's boyfriend comes in, carrying grocery bags.

"Will you sign my shirt?" she asks.

I take the pen from her hand and write my name on the back of a Shit Happens T-shirt.

"And my hand?" she asks, shyly.

I'm signing her hand when the boyfriend comes to interrupt this scene.

"Let's go," he says, glaring at me.

This is Tom, the guy I fought with at the D. The girl looks at her hand, the shirt.

She smiles. "I think you're great."

"We're out of here," Tom says. She turns around, gathers her clothes, and walks out the door. Mikey's outside, smoking a cigarette.

"*Top Gun* sucked," Tom says as he leaves. "Believe it."

Louis looks at me and shrugs. "Good thing you weren't in it."

"America loves him," Nathan says, still reading the instructions, "because he wasn't."

"There's nothing to it," Louis says, pointing to the washing machine. "Let me demonstrate. I have to say it's really kind of weird that you've never washed your own clothes. But considering what a ridiculous life you've probably led . . ."

Louis picks up the detergent box and pours what looks like way too much powder into the machine. "First you put in the soap. Then, depending on how picky you are about these things, you either separate your colors, or you're like me and you figure what the hell and put all the dirty clothes in together."

Louis dumps in his dirty laundry. Nathan watches carefully.

"I put all the colors in first, and then I put in my whites. Sort of separate them. That way, if what I learned in college is true, about heat rising, then all the hot water rises to the top of the machine, where all your whites are."

Louis shuts the machine and puts coins in the slot.

"Whites get cleaner in hot water," Louis says. "I saw it on a commercial." Louis speaks slowly, stressing each step. "Then you put in your money, push the start button, light a cigarette, marijuana or tobacco, whichever you prefer, or whichever you have. Inhale, exhale. And you repeat those last steps until you hear the buzzer."

Nathan scratches his head, sort of confused.

"It may take days, but eventually you'll hear the buzzer," Louis says, adding, "You helpless moron."

Danny is now videotaping himself putting his clothes in a dryer.

I light another cigarette. Mikey comes in from outside.

Danny points the camera at us. "Does one of you guys have a quarter? I need a quarter. I'm one shy."

"What do you need it for?" Louis asks.

"Becky's rates for a blow job have gone up a nickel?" Danny says. "What do you *think*, shithead?"

Louis reaches into his pocket, pulls out a handful of change, and throws a quarter at him. Danny ducks. The quarter misses his head, hits the wall, and rolls around. Danny tries to follow it with the camera, unfazed.

"You have to aim for the head," Louis says, red-faced.

"All the old plaster goes," Jeremiah says to the workmen. "All of it."

Jeremiah surveys the walls, wood frame being exposed by three guys in jeans and workboots. Danny pans across the room with the camera, then points it at me.

"Are you going to sell this place after you fix it?" Danny asks.

"And do what?" Jeremiah asks. "And live where? Santa Monica? Hollywood?"

"Yeah," Danny says. "Go back."

Monty walks by, comes back, and enters.

"I'm never going back," Jeremiah says. "*Never*. I'd rather live in an igloo."

"You shouldn't have to," Monty says. "That was a pretty fat check I wrote you."

"Selling out," one of the workmen says. "Shit."

"Hey. Watch it," Jeremiah warns.

"Don't think of it as selling out," Monty says. "Think of it as two extra years away from your old man."

"Good point," Jeremiah says, relaxing.

"Danny," Monty says. "Word around here is that you have extensive footage on Emery."

"That is the fact." Danny points the camera at me.

"I was thinking we should talk," Monty says. "I'll put you in touch with the unit publicist. Maybe we could take some of it off your hands."

"I'm going to assume that you'll be paying top dollar for it, Monty," Danny says, camera still aimed at me. "Or else I'm going to assume you're incredibly naïve."

Jeremiah lights a cigarette.

"No problem," Monty says. "We'll work something out. I think we can use some of it for our EPK. Severely edited, if you get my drift. That bit with Danielle trying to persuade our little friend Emery with, shall we say, amorous ammunition for starters." Monty looks at me and smiles. "You are a very bad boy, Emery." Monty leaves.

"Monty says that I have talent," Danny says, camera now back to the workmen.

"Monty says everybody has talent." Jeremiah inspects a loose wire.

"Maybe you'll be in my first movie," Danny says to me, putting down the camera.

"This is probably the smartest thing Emery has ever done, taking off," Jeremiah says. "His price is going to sky-rocket. Watch."

"Emery?" Danny asks. "Is this true?"

"I'm tired," I say.

Jeremiah picks up a hammer and hits a hole through the wall, pulls away some old plaster. "From now on, if you want Emery in your movie, you're going to need real money." Jeremiah slams the hammer through the wall again. "If you want Emery, you're going to need a blank check."

I sit in the chair with my name on the back. It is higher than anyone else's, except for Monty's, and I literally have to climb onto it. The crew sets up another shot because Briston wants to do it again. This woman, I don't know who, is talking to Danielle and the unit publicist, Judy. They are speaking very fast, though I can't hear what anyone says. Danielle looks at me, keeps talking, and then they all look at me but try not to. Danielle holds up a finger to them: Stay put.

"You don't have to do this," Danielle says, putting her hands on my thighs. "But it would be nice."

Briston's son, Briston Jr., arrived last night, and he walks over and hands me a cigarette, then lights it.

"How are you faring?" Briston Jr. asks, then, nodding: "Danielle."

Danielle says, "I need to have a word with Emery."

Briston Jr. leaves. Danielle rolls her eyes.

"This is what happens when you can't insure the director because he's too old," Danielle says. "Monty's paying Briston Jr. something like a half a million to finish the picture if Briston dies or something."

"Is Briston going to die?" I ask.

"She wants to interview you for the piece," Danielle says impatiently.

"But is Briston going to die?" I ask.

"Baby?" Danielle says. "Please. The piece. Focus. Focus. Calm blue ocean. Calm blue ocean."

"Cover?" I ask.

"*New York Arts,*" Danielle says. "She's the only one Monty's let on the set, and she leaves tonight. I don't know about the cover."

"Let her leave," I say. "What's her name?"

"Bettina," Danielle says. "Worth."

"I don't like her name," I say. "I don't like the name Bettina."

"Bettina Worth is going to write the piece whether Emery Roberts talks to her or not," Danielle lies.

"Tell her to talk to my sister," I say. "Julia."

"She's going to play up all of this disappearance stuff with you," Danielle warns.

Danielle takes my hand and looks at my nails, shiny from this morning's manicure.

"I know it's stupid," she says, gesturing around the set. "All of this is stupid."

"I don't get it," I say.

"Why the movie is a piece of shit?" Danielle asks, confused. "What don't you get?"

"No," I say. "I-just-don't-get-it."

Danielle takes my face in her hand and squeezes. "Emery Roberts doesn't have to get it," she says, kissing me lightly on the chin. "That's the beauty of this. Emery Roberts doesn't have to get it."

Danielle waves to Bettina and Judy. Dmitri taps me on the shoulder.

"Emery," he says. "Some of the people want to meet you? Okay?"

"Time to placate the masses." Danielle smiles understandingly.

Someone pins a red AIDS ribbon to my shirt, and I turn

around and look at the thirty or so fans waiting at a roped-off area.

"Come," Dmitri says. "Soon. Please."

"Dmitri," Danielle says. "You're speaking Korean. Chill. Emery will come-soon-please shortly."

Dmitri walks away, toward the people.

Danielle says, "I can't understand a word he ever says."

I sigh. "He's Irish."

"Oh, good. Then he can be of help to Becky. With that screenplay she's developing with Googie and Huggie," Danielle says.

"It's about a potato famine," I say. "Becky's screenplay is about a potato famine, Danielle."

"Baby, the movie you're making right now is based on a short story by a group of fifth graders from Santa Cruz," Danielle says softly.

"Whatever," I mutter.

Danielle points with her head toward the writer. "Baby?"

"I don't want to," I say. "Feeling nauseous."

"Of course you are." Danielle moves closer, speaking softly. "I thought maybe since we have the next two or three days off, we could drive south of here, on excursion. Norman has invited me and some friends to spend the weekend in a place called Pownal," Danielle says, checking her Filofax. "Norman Lear."

"Who's that?" I ask.

"You and me and friends at a big country house? You must be sick of this dump. The water runs brown most of the time. Electricity's iffy. People everywhere."

"The movie people stay at the Ramada," I say, staring off into space, vaguely aware of Danielle's presence.

"Baby," Danielle says. "Are we—are we—you know . . ."

"Please, Danielle," I say. "If you're going to ask me a lame question, at least make it quick."

"I just want to know if things are still the same between us." She breathes in.

"Emery?" someone says. "Let's go. We're on here."

Six different people yell for quiet.

"Oh, God," Danielle says, spotting someone.

"Danielle," I say.

"Rising actor from sitcom hell, whose name is Erich Philbin or Phildorf or something, is going to come up and pat you on the back," Danielle says.

"Go to it," Erich says, smiling nervously, patting me on the back.

"Are you done for today?" Danielle asks. "You look great, really."

Erich nods. "Briston really loved me today." Erich moves over to the ropes.

"Hear those sighs of gratitude from the masses?" Danielle asks, tilting her head.

Dmitri appears. "Autograph people will wait for you."

"Erich is going to be big," Danielle murmurs. "If he loses about ten pounds. Face is a little too round."

I walk in front of the camera. I'm lit, repositioned. Makeup puts last touches on my face.

"No rehearsal," I hear Hurley saying. "I want to see how this comes out cold."

"No rehearsal?" Briston asks, playing along. "What do you mean?"

"What part *didn't* you understand?" Hurley asks.

"I am the director, I am the hand of God. You are the talent, you are a tool. Do I really need to remind you of this? You haven't any say in the matter, and we'll rehearse as I see fit. There'll be none of this," Briston says. "I'll be in my trailer. You're all a crashing bore."

"Monty," Hurley whines. "I can't work like this."

Monty pulls Hurley aside, and Briston glares at me.

Some of the fans wave over Erich's head, bent low, signing autographs. Hurley manages to give the finger to the crowd. A girl squeals, gratified.

Monty comes back from talking with Hurley.

"Let's just wrap for today." Briston sighs. "Hurley's a little hung over and doesn't seem to be in the mood for me. And to tell you the truth, for once I'm not in the mood for him. There's not a script in the universe that little shit can hide behind. Deliver me, Monty. Deliver me from pissy actors."

"We're already three days behind schedule," Monty says. "Not to mention Emery's fuck-up. So I don't think it's that good an idea."

Squeals, girls scream my name.

Briston sighs. "Yes, Emery, you are beloved. Unaccountably, I might add, but beloved nonetheless."

Briston takes the script from Monty and flips through it. When he finds the spot, Briston rips out three pages and drops them to the ground. Dmitri attempts to pick them up, but Briston stops him with his foot.

"That should put us back on track," Briston says. "And I'm *not* taking the piss out of you here, Monty."

Later Nathan comes running up with a shovel in his hand, after flashing a laminated pass at security.

"Monty," Nathan says, out of breath. "The teamster guys say they'll help me dig. Twenty bucks an hour extra. Think you can swing it?"

"Each?" Monty asks.

"Oh, Christ." Briston sighs. "What do *you* think?"

It has been raining pretty much all morning. The pool hole is nothing like it should be. The bottom is full of water, mud, sticks, leaves. Nathan and Louis try to do what they can, but the pool gets bigger and the rain falls so hard and constantly that they have to stop and go inside. Jeremiah has hired about twenty of the carpenters to help fix the house: hammering, sawing, noise. People from production roam everywhere. Lines for the phones even though it's Sunday. After a two-hour workout with Monty's personal trainer, I'm in my room, where I take off soaking wet clothes and stare at the ceiling. I fall asleep for a while, and when I open my eyes, Danielle is standing by the window, wearing a unitard, sweaty, holding a Filofax. I pull the sheet up over my head. She lights a cigarette, talks.

"I work out," Danielle says. "I smoke. I work out, I smoke."

Danielle opens the window, tosses the cigarette out in the rain.

"Did you go to aerobics?" I ask from underneath the sheets. "In the big room?"

"Monty's trainer is so in shape it's sick," Danielle says.

"I'm a fucking basket case," I say.

"You leave your door unlocked," Danielle says.

"That's because there's no lock on it," I say carefully.

Danielle pulls the sheet away from my face and I close my eyes.

"Don't worry, baby," Danielle says. "Trying to fuck you to get you to cooperate—well, that plan doesn't seem to have any effect." Danielle sighs, blows smoke rings. "I shouldn't be surprised."

"I like . . . Anne," I hear myself say.

"What's going on?" she asks, tapping my forehead lightly. "What's really going on in there?"

"Guess," I say.

Everyone is in a bad mood. Monty, Hurley, Danielle, Briston. The rain hasn't let up for four days, and all we can do is wait. Hurley flew a chanter, a guru in from Bangkok, to put a spell on the clouds, to make the rain stop. Her name is Maya or Mina (depending on the time of day), and she wears a lot of orange, has a shaved head, and when I'm outside watching Nathan dig the pool, she stares up at the sky, lights fires, sprinkles spices onto the ground, demands that a satellite dish be installed to catch Dodger games.

A bunch of us pack into two cars and drive down to the Suzanna Lanes, which on this Saturday night Monty has rented out. Danny brings his camera and tapes everyone bowling, long sweeping shots of the alleys. Locals stare from outside, through the windows. Monty actually considered putting up venetian blinds but let it go. The shy couple who owns Suzanna Lanes tries to start a conversation, but Monty tells Mikey to keep them away.

"It's been forever since I went bowling with my kids." Monty did not want to come.

Jeremiah nods grimly. Anne examines a blue ball to see if her thumb fits right.

"Millions of Americans bowl every weekend," Danny says, narrating.

Louis throws a pencil at Danny's head. "Direct hit," Louis says.

"Your turn, Emery," Anne says. "Emery? Emery, hello? I said it's your turn."

Hurley says, "Maya told me that my team would win tonight."

"Honey," Monty says to Anne. "Tell Hurley that the producer's team always wins."

"The producer's team always wins. Jesus, where are the drinks?" Anne says.

"You'll choke," Briston Jr. says, coughing. The rumor of "heroin addict" has been confirmed. The rumor of "HIV positive" has not.

"Do they even have bowling in England?" Louis asks sarcastically.

"It's originally a European sport," Briston Jr. says, dark circles under his eyes, long-sleeve shirt, black, just in case. "Bloodstains," Danielle whispered to me over dinner at The Inn.

"The British," Anne mutters, looking for a waitress. "Always *so* charming."

Danielle sits on one of the benches, not bowling, chain-smoking, scribbling into her Filofax. She dials a call on her cellular. The only word I can hear distinctly between pins falling is "friction."

I look at the score sheet and try to figure out what's going on.

"What does Emery need?" someone asks.

"A personality?" Monty suggests. "A real job?"

With great purposefulness Anne studies the score sheet.

"I don't think you should worry about all of this," Briston Jr. says in monotone. "Bowl for fun."

"Bowl to win," Monty says. "You kids today know nothing. *Nada.*"

"A strike," Louis says, looking at the score sheet. "A strike would do it here."

"I don't like that word mentioned when teamsters are around," Monty warns.

"But you're up against Dmitri," Briston Jr. says, absentmindedly playing with Becky's knees. "And all Dmitri needs is a spare and he's European and you haven't got a chance."

"Say Jaguar," Becky says to Briston Jr.

"Jag-u-ah," Briston Jr. says.

Becky giggles, flirting. "Okay, now say George Bernard Shaw."

"George Bernard Shaw," Briston Jr. says, unsmiling.

"Who's George Bernard Shaw?" someone asks.

"Starred in *Jaws,*" Louis says, glaring at Becky.

Louis has to lift my arm to high-five me.

Someone has to help me step into the lane. While I am looking for my ball, Louis gets the waitress's attention and holds up his beer and five fingers. The waitress nods, then looks at me.

Anne notices. "Ooh. A tingle."

Hurley taps me on the shoulder. "Don't mean to burst your bubble. I know confidence is a serious thing, half the battle. But I've seen Dmitri bowl. He's the best bowler you'll ever know. And this is competition, aggressive and pure. I've been dead twice, Emery. I know all about it."

Dmitri steps up and chooses a bowling ball. "You first, Emery. Please." He gestures toward my lane.

"Nathan's going to wish he was here," Louis says. "When Nathan hears how Emery beat the odds, saved the day, he's going to wish he was here to see it."

"Positive visualization, Emery," Hurley says. "That's the way to play it. Wars ought to be fought this way. No blood, no destruction. Just *mano a mano.*"

Louis says, "Go ahead, Emery. Just fucking bowl. Just one pin."

"Whenever you are ready," Dmitri says.

I swing the ball, let it loose, and it rolls down the side of the lane into the gutter. No one says anything. I wait for the ball to come back and let it roll again without thinking, and only two pins fall.

"Don't sweat it," Louis says, a real edge in his voice. "At least you try, right?"

"He got two pins," Monty says. "That's one better than we thought."

"I was dead," Hurley says. "Twice I've been dead and pulled back. And you know who did it? Maya. Maya reached over to my head, electricity flowed from her hand and sparks and various forms of energy, and Maya pulled me back. I was on a stretcher at Cedars-Sinai and Maya walked me out of there." Hurley pauses. "Then we had a quesadilla at Trumps."

"This is good?" Monty asks. "This is good news?"

"Better than good," Hurley says. "I'm alive."

"I believe that is open to interpretation," Louis says.

"Oh, Christ," Hurley says. "Can't you have a little compassion for anyone, you piece of shit?"

Monty tips the waitress for beers.

"He still needs a good roll to win," Anne says, watching Dmitri.

Dmitri bows and then gets into a bowling stance. Anne sits on my lap. This causes Danielle to look up, still on the phone.

"This is . . . not good," I say, trying to shift Anne's weight. Anne holds a glass of vodka in front of my face and tries to feed me a sip, but it runs down my chin. I sigh as she wipes it off.

"Sorry," Anne says, on the verge of tears.

"This," Dmitri says, "this is going to have to call for the two most secret bowling techniques known to man."

"What?" Louis asks. "An arm and a pulse?"

"George Bernard Shaw," Becky says in a fake English accent.

"Yow," Jeremiah says.

"Overhand aerial power bowling," Dmitri says. "For the strike. To clinch."

Dmitri backs up, then runs toward the line and throws the ball as hard as he can. It sails and lands on the wood, maybe halfway down the lane. It makes a loud sound, kind of bounces, and hits pins, all but one.

I push Anne off my lap. She wanders over to sit with her father, thinks again, moves away.

"Never said it worked one hundred percent," Dmitri says, shaking his head.

Danny says from behind the camera, "Dreams come cheap in this town, promises even cheaper."

"If I ever come in contact with another USC film student," Louis says, "one of us will not survive the meeting."

"For the spare," Dmitri says. "The secret weapon number two."

"Hex," Monty says. "Hex hex hex."

"Won't work, Monty," Hurley says. "Dmitri's seen it going down. The pin's already fallen, more or less. No hex in the universe can fight through that force. Nothing undoes future history."

"What's number two?" Monty asks. "What's secret weapon number two?"

"Ancient Dutch Finesse Bowling," Dmitri says, holding the ball over his head and doing knee bends.

"Old people are a drag," Louis says.

Nathan comes back from the bar, holding a trayful of Sea Breezes. Louis jumps up.

"What's going on?" Nathan says. "What happened? Did we win? Emery, there are a lot of young girls out there that want you. Badly. When I asked, they said, yes, they would fuck you for a quarter."

Casually Anne sips a Sea Breeze. "Emery, do you have a quarter?"

"No, Anne," Nathan says. "*They* would pay Emery a quarter." Then, under his breath, "You blithering idiot."

Dmitri stops his knee bends, continues to hold the ball over his head.

"I learned this in Africa," Dmitri is saying.

"Didn't know they bowled over there," Louis grumbles.

Dmitri takes two steps toward the line, pumps the ball over his head twice, lowers it with both hands, and lets it roll, slowly. It takes awhile to get there, but the pin goes down. Dmitri holds up his fist.

"Bravo," Briston Jr. says, eyes half closed.

"Jaguar," Becky says, drunk. "George Bernard Shaw."

"What are you doing here?" Louis asks Briston Jr. "You can't actually *like* hanging out on set."

"It's called getting paid," Briston Jr. says, licking his lips with anticipation. "Something, I hear, you're not terribly familiar with these days."

"What *are* you doing here?" Louis looks at Briston Jr. "Are you still a Scientologist or are you back to dealing?"

"I don't look at my life as either/or," Briston Jr. says.

"What about when you were taking those Self-Discovery Through Journal Writing seminars?" Louis lights a joint.

"There are people who would walk across garbage to be where you are, Emery," Briston Jr. says, sticking the needle in his arm. "Hell, to even touch you."

"Is that what you did?" Louis asks. "Walk across garbage to be with Emery?"

Briston Jr. undoes the belt from around his arm. "Figuratively."

We break for lunch, and everyone sits in the tent that has been set up in the front yard. I play with pasta salad, broccoli. In the corners of the tent are purple bug zappers. Mosquitoes light up, spark, die.

"Hurley was telling me about his channeler," Erich Phildorf says, then adds good-naturedly, "What a psychotic."

"Emery's better off not knowing," Louis says. "Stupid California shit."

"They sit in a room and contact the dead," Erich says. "The dead person, always famous by the way, contacts you through the channeler. They actually get inside the channeler's body and the channeler speaks through them."

"Have you ever contacted someone through a channeler, Em?" Louis asks.

"Now why do you think," Erich asks, "that the dead only contact people in the entertainment industry?"

"Do you really think a question like that deserves any attention?" Louis asks. "Christ, Erich. How many years have you been doing soaps?"

"May I?" Erich takes a piece of my broccoli. "I mean, why don't they contact real estate developers or venture capitalists?"

"You know what it takes to be a huge star?" Louis asks, then answers, "A big head."

"An ego?" Erich asks.

"No," Louis says. "I mean, a big head. A head of disproportionate size to one's body. Look at all the biggest stars. Huge heads, all of them. Christ, look at Emery's *head*."

Erich examines my head, then feels his own, looks uncomfortable.

"What's . . . a venture capitalist?" I ask. I have taken six Valium this morning.

Louis says, "Here comes Hurley."

Hurley and the DP sit down with their plates.

"Where's the guru?" Erich asks.

"Do you see any rain?" Hurley says. "Hasn't been a drop all day. Maya left for London. Andrew Lloyd Webber called. An emergency."

Louis says, "I think maybe Maya jumped the gun. Clouds out there look pretty bad. And by the way, has anyone ever told you, Hurley, that you have an enormous head?"

"The light," the DP says. "This is the *best* kind of light. Cinematographer's wet dream."

"Did you see the new set?" Hurley asks. "Briston and Monty had fifty men working up at that clearing by the lake. Only took them four days."

"What'd they build?" Erich asks.

Hurley doesn't look at him, speaks to me. "It's really quite extraordinary."

"What, Mr. Big Head?" Louis asks. "A commissary?"

"They built a house up there." I sigh.

"A whole house?" Louis asks.

"In this business," the DP says, "budget problems seem almost secondary on a project of this scope."

"Spending it," Hurley says, stuffing food into his mouth, jaw muscles straining. "Getting it back is another story."

"There's a house at the lake now?" Louis lowers a long strand of angel hair into his mouth.

"Spanish adobe," Hurley says. "It's something."

Another mosquito fizzles on the purple bug machine.

Dmitri comes into the tent, calling, "Okay, people. Time."

"I haven't *touched* lunch," Hurley says, mouth full. "Doesn't he know that?"

"I think you should sue," Louis says. "You and your giant head."

"I'm glad we're finally working again," Erich says. "I was on Will Notify for a month. This is better."

Hurley stops chewing and looks at Erich, then back at his food.

"Time, gentlemen," Dmitri says to our table. "Emery, makeup wants to see you very fast before we shoot this one."

"Lunch hasn't been fifteen minutes," Hurley says. "Goddammit, Dmitri."

"I know, Hurley," Dmitri says, rubbing Hurley's shoulders. "Please, now. It will be raining again soon."

"Maya assured me that it *wouldn't*," Hurley says, standing up.

Dmitri says, "We're working now. Five minutes. Up at the lake."

"I could go for a swim," the DP says. "It's so hot."

"Sounds good," Hurley says.

"Yeah," Erich says. "I could swim."

"Have you been to the lake, Emery?" the DP asks.

"Deal," Hurley says, only concentrating on his plate. "We swim at the lake after the scene today."

Louis glances at me, mouths "Let them."

"Will you join us?" Hurley asks. "You, too, Louis?"

Louis says, "I think Louis will pass. Louis promised to help with the pool."

"The pool?" The DP looks confused.

"They're building a swimming pool." Hurley snorts, eats some broccoli.

"That is the big hole in back? Whatever for?" the DP asks. "There is a beautiful lake."

Hurley says, "I can't wait in this heat for you boys to build a pool. Lake's good enough for me."

"Let's look alive, people." Dmitri comes into the tent again, clapping. "Even if we don't feel it, let's look alive, people. Ladies, gentlemen, please. Before we lose the light."

I get out of my chair, and someone takes off my robe and hands me thirty-pound barbells. I pump twenty curls on each arm and do two sets of thirty push-ups. Makeup sprays water mist on my face and chest, wets my hair. My shoulders kind of hurt, and I'm guided to the porch of the hacienda. Walkman head-phones are placed on my ears and I sit in a rocking chair.

"Now, Emery," Briston says. "Hurley's going to storm onto the porch here, and remember, he's furious with you. *Furious.* But you're calm. You just listen to your music, maybe tap your foot to the rhythm. Stay calm. Do *not* react."

"No problem," I say.

"When the shooting starts," Briston says, "it's time to duck and cover."

Three people yell for quiet.

"Quiet please," Dmitri says. "Quiet. Rolling."

"Speed," someone says.

"Entertain me," Briston says.

Hurley rushes onto the porch and looks around suspiciously.

"Where the hell have you been?" Hurley says. "The Colombians are pissed off."

I look straight ahead, tap my foot though there is no music coming from the headphones.

"They'll be here any minute," Hurley says, slamming his hand against a wall. "And you're listening to music?"

I tap my foot, nod my head.

"Weasel says we need to get ready for them," Hurley says. "They've got the . . ." Hurley stops, exhales, looks at his feet. "Line?" Hurley asks.

"Cut," Briston groans. "Cut, cut."

"I'm sorry," Hurley says. "Line please."

Someone says, "They've got the *codes*."

"That's eleven takes," Briston says. "Eleven, Hurley. And it's not Weasel, it's *Wendell*. Since when is there anyone named Weasel in this fucking picture?"

The party for Hurley is in the living room. We all raise our glasses. Monty is wearing a tux and makes a toast.

"To one year," Monty says. "It's not the day you were born, but it's sort of like a birthday. We're glad you're still around on a day that you might not have seen. Okay?"

"Hear hear." Briston smirks. "Hear hear."

Someone puts on music, a soul band.

Anne pours herself champagne. Anne started drinking at lunch. It is now eight.

"You ever try to kill yourself, Emery?" she asks.

"Not in the last few weeks or so."

"Me neither," Anne says, sipping champagne.

"It's good that you're . . . not an actress," I say genuinely.

Gladys plays with Enzo, kissing the baby on the nose. The kid's arms are flailing all over the place and he's crying. Briston Jr., sweaty, makes dumb faces at the kid, scaring it. Louis whispers something to Becky and she glares at him, resumes flirting with Monty. Louis tries to make faces at Enzo, too, but the baby slaps him in the eye. Briston Jr. and Gladys laugh. Louis moves to the bar and pours Stoli into an empty champagne glass.

"Here comes the guest of honor," Anne says. "I have to split. Can't deal."

"Don't leave me alone with him," I want to say, but she's already gone.

Hurley has two glasses of champagne and is heading my way. Hurley looks at me for a long time before speaking. "My costar," he says, mock-admiringly.

"I am," I say.

"Maybe I had the right idea," Hurley says. "Maybe it's time for the holy in this world to leave." He points up. "Out there is where we should put our stuff. That's where the energy should go. Early."

"Upstairs?" I ask, confused.

Hurley finishes a glass of champagne and puts it down. He shakes his head as if to clear it. "I mean, out *there*. It'll end up there anyway, but maybe giving it a little push, like I did a year ago. Maybe that's the thing to do. The way of the holy in an unholy world."

"But we're glad you're alive, Hurley," I say. "I mean, right? Aren't we?" Turning around, I realize that no one else is standing with us, so I rephrase: "I mean, right?"

Hurley nods. "I'm not talking about me. I'm speaking in a general sense." He gestures with his hand, at the room, at everyone.

"Are you . . . all right? Did you go swimming?" I ask. "At . . . the lake?"

"Strangest thing," Hurley says, nodding, looking around the room. "My advice is don't swim there."

"Xanax makes me . . . want to sleep," I say slowly, nodding.

"You have to understand, as a young man, because I was a young man once, the possibilities of making it out with anything that's worth anything are small. And if you're constantly thriving, constantly trying to *take* something out with you when you pass on, you'll *drown*. I know. I've been dead. Twice." Hurley says all this to me.

"You told me," I say. "You told me . . . more than twice."

"I know it's hard to think a perfect universe could have a no win," Hurley says. "But it does."

I nod and look around the room for Louis, for anyone. Danielle joins us.

"Danielle," Hurley says, "I was just telling your boy-friend here—"

"He's *not* my boyfriend." Danielle laughs. "Isn't that right, honey?"

"People don't have the time or the sanctity to grab all

they can get and I'm not talking about things *here,* you understand. The people who don't have the time should just take that shortcut, that easy route to nobody knows where, you know?"

"Should kill themselves?" Danielle finally asks. "You wouldn't be here making the big bucks if you had succeeded in that, now would you?"

"Not me. Others. Should go out there, maybe slightly unprepared, maybe others have an edge, but there's really no competition, see, so the tools will come sooner or later. Until then it's just floating toward the lights."

"Bright lights?" Danielle asks. "Heaven lights? Klieg lights?"

"The lights."

"What are you talking about?" I ask tiredly. "Hurley, please."

Hurley puts his hand on my shoulder. "I'd rather be *there.* But Maya says I've got some purifying to do on this plane. I'm unholy. I've got to work at it. But if given the choice, I don't know. Down here you've got trees and water and rocks and contracts and life. Out there you've got everything else. I need more champagne."

Hurley walks to the bar.

Danielle fidgets. "Oh, my." She watches Hurley. "He's been attending a lot of, um, Marianne Williamson seminars."

"Oh, fuck, Danielle," I moan. "You don't have to defend Hurley Thompson to me."

AJAY SAHGAL

"It's your birthday next week," Danielle says. "What are you going to do?"

I shrug, finish my champagne. "Get older?"

"Such a cool answer." Danielle walks away.

I see Monty on the phone. He yells into it: "Julia Roberts is *not* interested in doing a script about *ice*, Manny . . . No . . . This is firsthand information from Joe Roth's mouth to my ears, okay?"

Louis hands me another glass of champagne.

"Emery's having creature trouble?" Louis asks.

I look around the room.

"I think it's good to hate people," Louis says. "A good healthy hate."

"What's happening?" I ask.

"Steve Danalon?" Louis asks. "Know him?"

It takes me too long to say, "Could."

"Killed," Louis says. "On dead man's curve there by Will Rogers Park. Another idiot in a Porsche dies on Sunset."

"I don't know him," I say. "I didn't know him . . . Blond?"

"I'm not going back," Louis says, making a face. "L.A."

Anne taps me from behind. I turn around.

"Is he gone?" Anne says.

"No Hurley here," Louis says, then asks Anne, "Did you know Steve Danalon?"

Anne shakes her head. "What did Hurley want?"

"Died in a car crash," Louis murmurs. "Dead."

"I didn't understand a word," I say. "Something about the universe."

"Hurley is creepy," Anne says. "Gorgeous, short, but creepy."

"Hurley chatted me up, too," Louis says. "Told me that everyone holy should think about killing themselves, moving on to the next . . . something."

"How fashionably bleak," Anne says. "Mr. Creepy."

Louis grabs a champagne bottle from Nathan.

Louis pours Nathan a glass and fills the rest of us up, too.

"Hurley told me about the suicide attempt," Nathan says. "Kind of scary."

"Drink," Louis says.

"Aren't you afraid to die?" Nathan asks.

Unsure of who he's asking, I shrug my shoulders.

"Drink your champagne," Anne says. "Shut up."

Nathan brushes something off his jacket. "I mean, it's all over then. And what did you do?"

"Just drink, Nathan," Louis says.

"What if you did nothing?" Nathan asks.

"The pool," Anne says. "There's your mark. Okay? Now shut up, you shithead."

"Aren't you afraid of dying, Louis?" Nathan asks.

Mikey is watching me. I smile at him. He bows his head.

Louis says, "I have survival instinct. I was born with it."

Nathan takes a sip of his champagne. *"That's* what made you such a crappy agent?"

Anne says, "For God's sake."

"So how'd Hurley do it?" I ask.

"Hurley took a hundred aspirin," Anne says. "Bayer. Children's. Chewable."

Danny comes up with the video camera and points it at Louis and Anne. Nathan moves out of the way, and the two of them stand as if posing for a still. Danny motions for us to move around.

"Act natural," Danny says. "Be yourselves. On second thought, try to be interesting."

Anne drunkenly covers the lens with my hand.

"A hundred aspirin," I say. "And then what happened?"

"And then what happened?" Anne finishes her champagne. "He threw up."

Louis and Anne and I watch TV. It's late, I'm tired, "Saturday Night Live," a tape of the show I hosted last year.

"This isn't very good," Louis says. "This isn't very good."

"It's not Emery's fault," Anne says. "Well . . . not exactly. Let's not think about it."

"I'm tired," I say.

Anne looks at her glass. "I'm turning in."

Louis stays and watches TV. Anne and I go upstairs. She

follows me to my room. I open the door. The room is completely empty. The walls are torn up, wires and nails everywhere. Anne checks the hall to make sure it's the right room.

"What's going on?" Anne asks. "Where's your stuff?"

Anne leads me down the hall to her room. She doesn't turn the lights on after she shuts the door.

"Someone put it all somewhere," she says, taking off her clothes and getting into bed. "The contractors."

"No one said anything," I say.

"They'll be done in a couple of days." She yawns, reaching for a prescription bottle. "You'll get it back."

I sit on the sill of the window, look out at the hole Nathan has dug. Kevin, the dog, roams the perimeters, sniffing. I light a Marlboro. Anne swallows two capsules, dry. A moth hovers in moonlight by the nightstand.

From Anne's bed: "Danielle wanted to know if you and I were seeing each other."

"What did you say?" I ask.

"I said, 'Is that a joke?' "

"Anne, I . . ." I start, can't finish.

"And then I asked Becky what happened out in Death Valley when—"

"Anne, I need—"

"—you started shooting—" She stops, breaks down. "Emery . . . you aren't possible . . . to me."

"Anne, I need you."

"Emery, you don't need because you can't." Anne sobs. "You can't need."

On the way home from the D, Louis stops at the hospital in town to get a cheeseburger.

"I rate it the best late-night place to eat in this town," Louis says, driving through the woods, chewing food. "The Suzanna Hospital cafeteria. Open twenty-four and three sixty-five."

"How did you find out about it?" Becky asks. "I don't think even Jeremiah knows."

"Zagat's." Louis.

"Doesn't anyone think Briston Jr. should perhaps check himself in?" Anne asks.

"Jeremiah knows nothing," Nathan says from the front seat, drunk. "Jeremiah knows home improvement. Only."

"He knows location fees," Louis says. "Jeremiah knows about that."

Nathan mumbles something. "No wonder Monty feels sonless."

Danielle leans up against me, and I feel kind of nauseous from the smell of the food Louis is eating.

"Are we fucking lost again?" Anne asks on my other side.

"I know exactly where we are," Louis says.

"Don't you wish sometimes that you lived in a small

POOL

town, or even a regular place? Seattle? Akron?" Nathan asks.
"That you had a job and a life and all that?"

Louis shakes his head.

"Todd Hill," Anne says. "Todd Hill Road, Louis. Right
turn."

Louis keeps driving. "Trust me. Stick with me here. This
is my neighborhood."

"You're not an agent anymore, Louis," Danielle says.
"So lose the spiel."

Anne takes the scotch bottle from Nathan and takes a
slug. She hands it to me, and I do, too.

"Is that good stuff?" Anne asks, eyes closed. "Or *what?*"

"Monty says you're going to win an Oscar," Danielle
says, squeezing my leg. "One day," and then: "Before you
die."

Nathan says, "I always wanted to go up on that stage and
hold that little gold bald guy in my hand, then take a leak right
there in front of millions of viewers from around the globe."

Outside, raindrops hit the windshield, little ones, and it
smells like trees and heat and water.

"I played pool with Googie and Huggie," Louis says.

Nathan mumbles, "Have to have good names to be good
screenwriters."

"Nathan doesn't cut it," Anne says. "Now if it was
Nordham or Nigel or Niblet, you'd have deals all over town."

"Why do you think he gave it up?" Becky asks. "Why do you think he's digging holes?"

Louis speeds up. "Nathan wants to leave a mark on the planet before he kicks it."

"I caught thirty-one turtles," Nathan says. "The confirmed number of turtle dead is now thirty-one."

"Congratulations," Anne says flatly.

"That doesn't count any that I injured with BBs, the ones that sank . . . or whatever."

"The MIA turtles," Louis says.

"Hardly a fucking dent," Nathan says. "I still see millions of them everywhere in the water. I see millions of them in my sleep."

"Louis," Anne says quietly. "We should be there by now."

"We're almost there," Louis says. "Hand me the Glenlivet."

Anne passes up the bottle, and Louis lights a cigarette, then takes two huge gulps. He cringes, shakes his head.

We come up on a slow-driving car. Louis flashes his brights.

"What's the deal?" Nathan says. "Pass the fuck."

"Ever play vigilante?" Louis asks.

Louis reaches under the dash and turns on the car alarm. Louis flashes his brights again. The car in front of us pulls over. We speed by.

"Big man," Anne says. "Barrel of laughs."

Louis turns off the alarm and makes a right onto a small dirt road.

"You and Becky got problems," Nathan says. "Saw her all over that Briston Jr. guy. *Little* Briston."

"I adore being discussed in the third person when I'm sitting right next to you," Becky says. "Jesus, Nathan. Who fed you that shit?"

"Becky has a tendency to fall for Eurotrash and 'neat-looking' heroin users," Louis says. "It happens that Briston Jr. is both."

"I've never once fallen for one," Becky says.

"What about that guy from Salamanca?" Anne asks.

"I think Anne has made my point." Louis sighs.

"I saw Anne blow a valet at Granita," Danielle says. "But that was when you were drinking four bottles of Absolut a day instead of—what is it now, honey? Three?"

"You're not upset?" Anne asks, ignoring Danielle. "Louis isn't even upset?"

"How can I be upset over *that* nothing?" Louis says.

Louis shrugs and hands me the bottle. I take another sip, close my eyes, getting the spins. Becky is totally silent.

"Am I shitty, you guys?" Nathan asks, slurring his words. "Am I a worthless piece of shit?"

"Worthless?" Louis asks. "No."

* * *

It rains all the time. I have the day off. Briston reshoots exteriors with Hurley and Becky. Louis and Nathan work on the pool all day. Mikey helps, too. Mikey is in what Nathan is calling the "deep end," hauling dirt over to a big pile. The hole is starting to look like a pool now except that it has no cement and no water.

"This is just like the Nam," Louis says.

"When are you shooting that big climax scene?" Nathan asks. "The chase through the hacienda?"

"It's done," Mikey says. "They did it last week."

Nathan nods.

"Emery needs a bath," Louis says. "He's dirty."

Danny comes out with the camera going, an umbrella attached to it.

"Emery never smells," Nathan says. "Emery might be dirty, but he never smells."

"He's a star," Danny says. "Stars don't smell. Emery's smell-less."

Nathan says, "I'm going to hunt turtles. Want to come, Danny?"

Danny makes the okay sign.

Nathan climbs out of the hole, and Danny follows him down the path to the lake, camera going.

Mikey feels the front of his shirt and coughs, goes inside. Anne comes out the back door, her hands flat, catching the rain. She walks over to Louis.

"Hey, birthday boy," she says to me.

Louis looks at me. "How come Emery didn't tell anyone?"

I say, completely surprised, "I forgot."

Anne squeezes my cheeks so hard that I have to pull away.

"Birthdays always get depressing," Anne says.

"How old are you?" Louis asks. "Take your time. It's a difficult question. Weigh your options."

I have no idea what to say.

Louis sighs. "I guess this needs to be translated to you by people you understand." Louis snaps his fingers. "Okay. Bring in the Muppets."

"Twenty-six," I say. "I think." I look at Anne.

"Yes. Twenty-six."

"Something quiet?" Louis suggests. "Maybe just the three of us? Dinner in town? Gladys made dinner, but we could eat at that steak place."

"I was watching 'Entertainment Tonight' just now," Anne says. "You have the same birthday as Cindy Williams, Valerie Harper, Tito Puente, and Monty Hall."

Anne wakes me up and gets me dressed. She throws some of my clothes in a bag and guides me unsteadily down the hall, reeking of scotch. She hands me four, five Klonopins, tells me in a hoarse whisper, "Take them."

Outside it rains and we get into Louis's car. Anne puts my seat belt on for me. She starts the car up, and we pull down the driveway with the lights off, complete darkness. On the road she finally turns on the lights and we swerve. Anne blinks a lot and tries to focus.

"I'm going to get you the hell out of here." Anne slurs her words, shakes her head to clear it. "Runaway time. You and me."

"Where?" I ask, swallowing another Klonopin.

"Anywhere," Anne says, sipping from a flask. "Away."

She hands the flask to me and I finish the last sip of vodka.

Anne drives for maybe five minutes, and rain hits the windshield. Anne's window is down and her face is getting wet. She rubs her eyes, nodding off. The headlights catch an animal, a squirrel, something covered with fur, and the car runs it over. A bump.

"What was that?" Anne slurs, tears in her eyes.

"I don't know," I say.

Anne looks in the rearview mirror. "Jesus, did I run somebody over? Jesus."

Up ahead is a curve, and Anne keeps staring in the rearview mirror, not turning.

"Anne," I say.

She looks forward and screams as we skid for a long time and hit the tree. I get out of the car and look at the smashed hood, steam rising from it. A tire is flat. It starts to rain harder, the car's headlights shooting straight ahead. I look in the car, and Anne's eyes are closed. She's drunk and sobbing.

"Anne," I say. "Are you all right?"

"Just go, Emery," Anne mumbles between gasps. "Just get out of here."

A few minutes later: red and blue flashing lights, and another car behind that.

Anne looks up, her eyes half open.

Monty comes up to my side of the car with a policeman, and Anne gets out and runs down the road, screaming. Mikey chases after her.

"If this is your idea of escape, you little bug," Monty says, grabbing my arm, "I have to tell you that it's pretty pathetic."

"Anne drove me," I say.

"You and Anne are *not* a possibility," Monty says. "There is *no* way that's going to happen."

I pull out a cigarette. The cop lights it.

"If you want a woman, that's what Danielle is for," Monty says. "I will *not* allow this other *thing* to happen. Do you hear what I'm saying?"

"Anne . . . likes me," I say.

"My daughter? My baby girl with *you?*" Monty says. "Nuh-uh. Are you fucking kidding me?"

* * *

Briston and Briston Jr. and Becky and Monty and Hurley and I are in Briston's trailer, watching dailies. I rub my eyes. Monty freeze-frames the tape.

"Bloody cut to the chase," Briston Jr. says. "Jesus, Becky, you look like shit."

Becky hits him in the arm. Monty rewinds a scene and replays it. Monty cracks up and claps, and Briston and Hurley are laughing, too. I look at the screen when Monty laughs and light a cigarette.

"Oh, Hurley." Briston sighs, staring at the monitor. "The way you deliver the money line. Gut-wrenching. As usual you were so much better than you needed to be."

"You're practically dead, Briston." Hurley scowls. "No one takes you seriously, you viper."

"Did everyone hear about Nathan's script?" Becky asks.

Hurley says, "That piece of shit about the ghosts?"

"It sold this morning," Briston says quietly. "The idiot savant got one-point-two for it."

"Emery, did you hear?" Becky asks.

"About . . . the haunted house?" I ask.

Briston says, "The ghosts of two whales, one friendly, the other not so friendly, live in a small house by the ocean. Their trials and tribulations lead them—inevitably—to open an espresso bar with the old salt that killed them." Briston pauses gravely. "The synopsis makes the script sound more coherent than it actually is."

"Oh, it sounds adorable," Becky says. "Anyway, Googie and Huggie have already been assigned to rewrite it."

"It's a staggeringly rotten piece of shit," Briston says. "I take that back. It's not a script. It's a scriptlike object."

"I happen to like it," Monty says. "I happen to think it dances."

"The thing makes no fucking sense whatsoever," Briston says.

"Meg Ryan is very interested in playing one of the whale-spirits," Monty says. "How bad could it be?"

Becky gets on the phone and starts to talk, giggle. Monty rewinds the tape again and we watch the scene. Again.

Becky covers the phone's mouthpiece and tells us the following: "Sofia Coppola had a wine tasting by the pool at the Château and Ione fell in the water." She returns to her phone call.

"Fascinating," Briston says, rubbing his eyes.

A knock on the door. Dmitri enters and speaks to Monty. "Ready, boss."

"Final scene," Briston says. "Emery? Hurley? How do you boys feel?"

"Let's do it," Hurley says. "Let's just finish the goddamn thing."

* * *

Outside, the shot is set up. Two cameras on tracks. Makeup does its last bit of work on me. Someone tells me where to stand. I look over my lines again. Cue cards, in case I forget my lines, are placed strategically around the set. Five people yell for quiet.

Dmitri says, "Quiet please. Rolling."

"Speed," I hear someone say.

Briston says, "Entertain me. Action."

"I told you, Rex," Hurley says. "That chick was bad news."

"Yeah, you told me a lot of things," I say. "And maybe you were right."

"You saved my life," Hurley says. "And I saved yours."

"So we're even." I hold out a hand.

"As even as we're ever gonna be," Hurley says, taking it.

"Partner?" I ask.

"Partner," Hurley says.

One take and Briston says, "Brilliant! Cut and print."

The whole crew is standing around, applauding unenthusiastically. Hurley takes a bow and races off the set. Someone hands me a glass of water. I finish it and walk over to the pool hole, while everyone else is hugging, shaking hands.

I stand at the edge and look in. There is water at the "deep end." I kick a rock into the puddle and watch it splash. Beneath the surface something small darts around.

Monty comes up behind me and puts his arm around my shoulder.

"When does your flight leave?" Monty asks.

I head up the path to the lake and before I get there I can see the huge Spanish-style house that Monty had built for the shoot, looming over the water, now the area's massive new focal point. Nathan is in the middle of the lake, in the boat, his gun pointed at the water. He doesn't see me as I make my way to the house (what the script refers to as the "hacienda"). As I open the front door, I hear Nathan's gun fire twice; the sound echoes.

Inside, there are only two rooms done, no furniture in them. When I try the light switch, nothing happens because there are no lights. I walk around the house for a while, floorboards creaking under my feet. Most of it is just frame and all the dimensions are too small. In back there are no walls. A big area has been cleared and there are deep marks in the ground where equipment sat. In the corner of one of the rooms, exposed to the outside because there isn't a fourth wall, is a cactus plant, and I try to poke my finger on one of the thorns, but it doesn't draw blood because it's plastic and hollow and weighs almost nothing, and I take it apart section by section, unscrewing it from its planter until there's nothing left.

A raccoon runs across one of the beams. I move to the

front of the structure and stare out a window at the lake. Nathan is on shore now, sitting on the ground, looking at the gun and cursing himself. There's a turtle next to him on its back. The house drowns the entire scene in shadow. The sky clears and Nathan gets up, leaves. The sun comes out and it starts to get hot out. The house creaks, the raccoon makes noises in the next room.

At the edge of the water I'm already sweating. It's getting hotter. I take off my clothes, my skin burning, and dip my feet in the water. The floor of the lake feels slimy, mushy. I lower myself into the water, and then I'm swimming, twenty feet from shore, thirty, forty. The water is cold. Nothing bites.

Later, back at the main house, it starts to rain again and I stand there, my clothes getting soaked, looking into the hole. The water is three, four feet deep, and a small turtle swims around. There are BBs stuck in its shell, and when I touch it with a shovel, the animal retreats inside. Then I spot another.

Rain. The last of the crew packs up their stuff. Trucks pull out of the driveway one by one. A white limo comes for Monty. Jeremiah says goodbye. This morning Monty signed me to a three-picture fifteen-million-dollar deal at Warner's. My clothes are soaked, and I can hear little splashes in the pool hole.

"Bet Emery's glad to see Monty go," Louis says, watching the limo disappear down the driveway.

"Emery hasn't seen the last of Monty," Danielle says. "Hardly."

Jeremiah says, "What the fuck else would Emery do? Think about it, Louis."

"But . . ." Louis shakes his head.

"Some people are, shall we say, *cut out* for this kind of thing," Danielle says, and then, looking at Louis: "And some just aren't." Danielle walks back into the house, passing Anne on the way out. Anne doesn't look at Danielle and comes over with a drink in her hand.

"Why do you suppose everyone's so mean to you?" Jeremiah asks Louis, trying not to smile.

"You don't have to," Louis says to me. "It's done."

"Like I said," Jeremiah says. "What *else* can Emery do?"

I look over at the pool hole. Nathan aims the BB gun into the hole and fires off a couple of rounds.

"I just wanted to get one more," Nathan says. "You know, for the road."

"Nathan's going back?" Danny asks. His camera has an umbrella attached to it.

"*Everyone* is going back," Jeremiah says. "Whether they want to or not. I need peace."

"What about Anne?" someone asks.

"Anne can stay," Jeremiah says, rubbing his chin.

Anne says, "I'm honored."

No one says anything for a while.

"You can check out anytime you like," Jeremiah says, "but you can never leave."

Anne finishes her drink, winces. "Oh, please."

"Roll credits," Louis says.

We are lost again, on the way home from the D. No one in the car seems to know where we're going. Nathan is in the front seat, not as drunk as Louis, who is driving way too fast.

"Make a left on Todd Hill this time," Danny says. "I'm telling you in advance."

"I know where we are," Louis says. "I know where we're going."

We pass Todd Hill Road.

Louis speeds up and turns off his lights. It's completely dark and we can't see the road.

"Turn them back on," someone finally says.

Danielle says, "Louis, don't make me beat the shit out of you."

Louis sips from his beer bottle, burps, then slams on the brakes. We skid for a while; then it gets bumpy. The engine dies. We are sort of in a ditch, facing sideways.

"I have to piss," Louis says, getting out.

"Can't this wait until we're home?" Danielle asks.

"That could be hours from now," Louis says.

He gets out of the car. I climb out of the backseat, away from Danielle.

"Don't take forever," Danielle warns.

I stand next to Louis and we say nothing. I'm drunk and my head is spinning. Nathan gets in the driver's seat and starts the engine. Louis gets behind the car to push it out of the ditch.

"Put it in second," Louis says. "Wheels go slower in second."

Louis leans up against the car, and it's hard to keep his footing on the loose gravel.

My feet slip.

"I'm going to work for Monty," Louis says, grunting. "Can't deal."

After I don't say anything, Louis says, "Something's wrong with you."

He keeps pushing on the back of the car and the wheels spin and nothing happens.

Louis says, "You got a better idea?"

"Emery, afternoon," Danny says. "Take three."

The camera is on a tripod. Danny claps his hands together in front of the lens.

"It's running, Emery. We're rolling here."

Finally Danny hits the pause button.

"Are you going to cooperate or what?" Danny asks.

The wall room is full of empty beer bottles, and someone has left a half-eaten pizza next to where I'm sitting. It doesn't look that bad.

Danny hits record again.

"Emery, afternoon. Take four." Danny claps his hands in front of the lens.

Danny is behind the camera, and he squints, looks through the viewfinder.

He makes circles with his hands. He wants me to talk, get it going.

"I don't know what to say. Give me sides. Give me lines."

Danny adjusts something behind the camera.

"Where are we?" Danny sighs.

"Vermont."

"Can you be more specific?"

"The wall room," I say.

"Why is this place called the wall room when all rooms have walls?"

"It's just . . . the wall room."

"Please elaborate," Danny coaxes. "You look stumped."

"It's the most . . . outstanding feature of this room?" I ask.

"The *wall* is the most outstanding feature of this room?" Danny asks.

Danny doesn't like this, looks at the bottles. He lights a joint.

He looks into the viewfinder again, making another adjustment.

"Why do you suppose it's one of the few rooms that Jeremiah hasn't redecorated?" Danny asks. "This is a new approach, okay?"

I shrug.

"Why don't you read us something off the wall, Emery."

Danny moves the camera, slowly to the corner. He focuses on graffiti scrawled in black pen.

"Read," Danny says. "Read it."

I read: "They kill Bob in Florida, they murder him, and we are destined to come to the same ends as Mr. Marley if we are not terribly careful. We live in a society where we cannot ignore the implications of the singsong rhythm of the day. Look out, up, and around."

"What do you suppose that means?" Danny asks, interviewing.

"I don't know."

"Well, what do you *think* it means?"

"Whoever wrote it just wrote it," I say.

Danny plays with the focus again.

There are other words written in small letters, red ink.

"Read what it says, Emery."

I read. "Foreign journalists please use lobby telephones."

Danny loses patience. "I'm hungry. Think Gladys could whip up some sandwiches?"

"Gladys left," I say. "Monty hired her as his cook."

"It doesn't matter. Answer the question."

"What question?"

Danny scratches his head, looks confused.

I look at the wall.

"New questions then," Danny says, patience lost.

"I . . . don't like being asked . . . questions."

"Humor me." Danny takes a hit off the joint, then puts it out. "Why are you here?"

I stare into the camera.

"Why are you here?" he asks. "Answer the question, Emery."

I pick up a pen and write on the wall:

planetearthisblueandtheresnothingIcando

"I don't know," I say.

"You've cost people millions of dollars. Why?"

"I don't know."

Danny rubs his chin and looks through the viewfinder again. "Why do you think you're here?"

Nothing. Silence. I read what's on the wall.

"That's it? Nothing?"

"No."

"No other reason? Anne maybe?"

"No."

"Ask me what my documentary is going to be titled," Danny says.

"What's your documentary going to be titled?"

"I'm deciding between *The Void Has Widened* or *Sad Sad Sad*," Danny says. "Louis is going to try to sell it to HBO for me."

Ten minutes pass. Danny paces, lights another joint.

"Ask me what my favorite color is." I sigh. "For Christ's sake."

"What is your favorite color?" Danny asks.

"Blue. Greenish blue. Teal."

Danny considers this. "Some people are homosexuals and they don't even know it, Emery."

"I'm not a homosexual."

"What do you really know about women?"

"Nothing."

"Why do you act?" Danny asks. "Don't tell me because you get to fly first class or because they made you."

Silence.

"What about Danielle? Is Danielle going to be your agent?"

"Ask my agent," I say.

"Pretty uncomfortable, aren't you, Emery?"

"It'll happen one way or another."

"What will happen?" Danny zooms in, focuses.

"It."

Louis comes into my room and sits down on my bed, lights a cigarette.

"I'm going to Alaska," Louis says.

"Seriously?" I ask.

Louis holds up three fingers. "Scout's honor."

"What are you going to do in Alaska?" I shut my suitcase and check to see if I've left anything in the room. There's not a lot to check. "ICM open a branch there?"

"Monty wants me to scout locations for this next project, *The Vegetarians*, only now it takes place in Alaska and the new working title is *Cannibal*." Louis pauses. "Googie and Huggie are—ah, forget it."

"What about . . . Becky?" I ask.

"She left. Jeremiah says she's left me for Willy Phildorf."

"Who?" I ask.

"Actor," Louis says. "I swear if Jeremiah wasn't so goddamn *big* and if his fucking father wasn't Monty, I'd kick his meathead ass."

"When are you going?" I ask, then: *"Cannibal?"*

Louis looks around. "Now." He shrugs. "Is Emery really going back?"

I shrug. "I think I have to."

"Is that your only bag?" Louis asks, pointing to my only bag.

"Yes," I say.

"That's cool, I suppose," Louis says, trying to blow smoke rings. "It's good that we sold all your stuff. Now you can get new stuff."

I check my fingernails.

"You ever been there?" Louis asks.

"To Alaska?"

Louis nods. I shrug.

"So how did you like the summer?" Louis asks.

I don't say anything except maybe "Hot."

"As far as summers go," Louis says. "I think this was a pretty good one."

Danny takes my bag downstairs. I follow him past all the newly done rooms. In the TV room, next to the VCR, is one of Danny's unpacked videotapes, marked "First Day—Arrival." I stick it into the machine and hit play.

On the TV fuzz turns to black stillness, which fades, and the screen fills with orange color. The old stone house fills the frame. The camera pans to the left, and I'm lit by the sunset of that first evening here at Jeremiah's, the dull yellow light on my face.

"Later," Louis says, popping his head into the room. "My parting advice to a young actor: If you're going to die young, ODing and car crashes are the way to go. Much more romantic . . . more romantic than, say, accidental drowning or getting bitten by a spider."

I hit pause, and the image of me in the middle of orange light, the huge and dark house in the background, freezes, still. I hear Louis's rental car start up, then head down the driveway.

I walk outside, and Danny hands my bag to the limo driver, who puts it in the trunk and opens the door, waiting for me to get in. In the back Danielle talks on the phone. I lean in.

"Go and talk to Jeremiah before we head out," Danielle says, smiling. "He said you should make Monty give you your deal money in hundred-dollar bills."

Jeremiah waits in the kitchen with a tool bag slung over his shoulder.

"I'm putting in a new kitchen floor," Jeremiah says.

"I'm going," I say.

"I packed you a lunch," he says. "But I can't find it."

He backs away and holds up his hand, turns and walks down the hall.

Upstairs in the wall room, I go to the window and look out. The pool hole is full of water and mud. Anne sits in the kiddie pool, sunglasses on, sleeping. I pick up a pen from the floor and write the only thing that comes to mind, which is

goodbye.

6

POOL